SHEPHERD

Catherine Jinks has published more than forty books for adults and children. She has won many awards including the Victorian Premier's Literary Award, the Aurealis Award for science fiction, the Adelaide Festival Award and the Davitt Award for crime fiction. Catherine is a four-time winner of the Children's Book Council of Australia Book of the Year Award and in 2001 was presented with a Centenary Medal for her contribution to Australian children's literature. She lives in the Blue Mountains of New South Wales.

Shepherd

CATHERINE JINKS

TEXT PUBLISHING MELBOURNE AUSTRALIA

textpublishing.com.au
textpublishing.co.uk

The Text Publishing Company
Swann House, 22 William Street, Melbourne Victoria 3000, Australia

The Text Publishing Company (UK) Ltd
130 Wood Street, London EC2V 6DL, United Kingdom

Published by The Text Publishing Company, 2019

Book design by Jessica Horrocks
Cover images by Vladimir Godnik/Getty and iStock
Typeset by Duncan Blachford, Typography Studio

Printed and bound in Australia by Griffin Press, part of Ovato, an accredited ISO/NZS 14001:2004 Environmental Management System printer

ISBN: 9781925773835 (paperback)
ISBN: 9781925774597 (ebook)

A catalogue record for this book is available from the National Library of Australia.

Prologue

I'M GOING to die.

My guts have turned to water. There's no end to the purge; it's like the cholera, though not as swift. I've seen folk die of the cholera. They turn blue and their eyes bug out.

There's no one here to close my eyes. I'll die like a dog and the dogs will eat my corpse.

Those berries have done for me.

It makes no sense because the blacks eat those berries. Whenever I've come upon a vine laden with the little orange balls, they're never lower than a man can reach. A bird wouldn't eat 'em from the ground up, nor an opossum neither. A kangaroo wouldn't leave human footprints in the dirt beneath the vine.

I'd a notion that the blacks had bellies like an Englishman's, but I must have been mistook. I should have listened to the warnings. Rowdy told me once that a friend of his, after seeing the blacks with palm pineapples, sampled a few of the seeds and died.

'Those folk aren't like us,' Rowdy said. 'They're iron-gutted, like dogs.' Perhaps he was right.

At home I always knew what to eat when. Dewberries in July. Sloes in September, though they were very tart unless you waited till after the first frost to pick 'em. Haws, hips, beechnuts, sorrel...there was so much to eat in the forests and the hedgerows.

When I first came here, I thought it a cruel affliction to walk through a wood and not know what bird was singing, or which plants were safe to eat. Now I understand it's more than an affliction; it's certain death.

I see nothing around me that I can properly name. Ferns. Vines. Bushes. Trees that shed their bark instead of their leaves. Flowers with spikes instead of petals.

I'm going to die wordless, in a lonely hollow in a strange land. I'm going to die among beasts that I don't understand and plants that have killed me.

If I close my eyes and let my mind drift, I can pretend I'm asleep in the watch-box, with the dogs nearby. If the dogs were here, they would protect me. I can almost smell 'em; almost feel their warmth against my back.

But it's dark. If they were here they'd be guarding the sheep, not me, because the sheep are more important than I am.

The sheep are the ones who plague my dreams, with their torn bellies and bloody haunches.

My duty is to the flock, always. Without it I'm nothing.

New South Wales, 1840

1

WHEN GYP'S bark wakes me, I'm in the watch-box. She must be barking at a beast because she sounds angry. If she were barking at a man she'd sound frightened.

This windowless watch-box is little more than an oversized coffin on legs. Its roof leaks and its walls are full of chinks but none of the gaps are big enough for me to see through. As for the square hole that serves as a door, it faces away from the sheepfold, towards the hut. We placed the box thus, Joe and I, to keep out the wind, which rarely blows from the west here in autumn. There's nothing shielding the door save a piece of weathered canvas.

Since I can't see what ails the dogs, I'll have to climb out. But at least the lantern's still alight, its glow faintly visible through the canvas. I can't have been asleep for long; no more than three hours, at a guess.

I grope about for the musket, which I always keep in the watch-box with me, uncocked. Muskets are safer than lanterns because lanterns can be knocked over. I'm small for thirteen, but it's so cramped in here that even someone my size could easily kick a lamp while sleeping.

I can hear three dogs, now. Gyp's yap is clean and sharp, Pedlar's low and gruff. The third dog is snarling—until suddenly it yelps.

Pushing aside the canvas flap, I clamber out of the watch-box and its funk of sweat and mildew. My lamp hangs from one of the four handles that stick out like wagon-shafts from the ends of the box. Whenever Joe and I have to carry it from one place to another, he complains that he might as well be a chairman. He's told me about the swells at home who used to be carried about in boxes on poles, when the roads in England were so bad that you couldn't use a carriage on half of 'em. His father was a chairman, he says, before a runaway horse broke his skull.

When I lift the lantern, I have a good view of the sheep-fold, which is made of wooden hurdles lashed together with ropes. The sheep inside the fold mill about, bleating anxiously. They know they're in danger. They can hear it. Smell it. They might even see it, despite the darkness.

But they can't feel it; not yet. If they could they'd be screaming.

'Gerrout! Get!' My voice, clogged with sleep, breaks on a high note. Over by the fence, Gyp and Pedlar have cornered a wild dog. Teeth snap. Eyes glint. A flurry of fur unleashes a howl of pain.

At least it's not a man. I'm told the blacks keep dogs, but I doubt there are blacks nearby. If there were they would have speared me by now.

'Get! Go on!' I'm closing in when the wild dog breaks free. He's not a pure-bred—his tail's like a whip—and he's fast. Too fast. Once I put down the lantern I have to raise my gun, cock the flintlock, aim, fire. All the dog has to do is run.

When I pull the trigger the explosion makes my ears ring and my teeth buzz. I have to step through a drifting cloud of smoke to pick up the lantern. I swing it this way. That way. This way again.

I must have missed the damn mongrel; there's no sign of it.

'Tom?'

Joe Humble's awake and peering through the doorway of our hut, which has no windows and no cracks in its slab walls, either, because Joe has filled every one. His bad chest keeps him away from cold draughts; you can hear the muck in his lungs when he speaks, all rough and rumbling. He says he's not consumptive, but he's so skinny and bent, with such hollow cheeks and deep-set eyes, that he might as well be. His eyebrows are in good health, though, thick and dark and thriving, for all that his hair and beard are wispy grey.

'What's amiss?' He's carrying a lantern and has wrapped a sheepskin around his shoulders.

'Dogs.'

'You sure o' that?'

I know what he's trying to say. He's worried Dan Carver'll come creeping back one night and slaughter us both.

'I saw one.'

'Lose any stock?'

I shake my head.

'Check the hurdles,' says Joe. Then he goes back inside.

He wants his rest and I can't blame him. The hut was built for three—two shepherds and a hutkeeper. But with Carver gone, Joe must tend the sheep as well as cook, clean, fetch water and move hurdles. That's why I've been sleeping in the watch-box lately, guarding the flock at night. Not that Joe ever used the watch-box, of course; he liked to doze against a tree at night, then nap during the day.

A hutkeeper can take such risks. No shepherd can.

The dogs are calmer now. Gyp stands guard, sniffing the air, as Pedlar weaves about with his nose in the dirt. Time to reload. Out comes the cartridge; I bite the paper at one end and tear it off. A pinch of black powder into the priming pan, then the rest ends up in the barrel beneath the musket ball, which I tamp down with a ramrod.

Gyp barks.

'I know. He's still out there.'

With the musket slung over my shoulder, I circle the fold, shaking each hurdle to make sure it stands fast. In the place where the wild dog was cornered some of the ropes are loose.

When I hunker down to look, there are dark splashes in the dirt.

'Gyp!' God ha' mercy, is she bleeding? I can't be sure until I've felt her coat, because she's black and white like all Scotch collies. But when I touch her black patches, she doesn't whine or flinch.

Pedlar, being a yellow mongrel, would show a blood-stain—and there isn't a drop on him.

'Did you get the bastard? Good girl.' Now that I look, I can see a trail of blood disappearing into the darkness. The wild dog must have been wounded when it ran. But how bad is the wound and how long the trail?

I'll find out tomorrow.

++

My dreams are never good. In my poaching dreams, I'm always caught. In my dreams about Ma, she's always on her deathbed. My father always beats me and my trial always ends on a hangman's rope. Sometimes I dream that the ship bringing me to New South Wales founders and sinks. Sometimes I dream that I'm being flogged.

I never have been flogged, but I've witnessed many a flog-ging. They stay with me. So do the faces of the dead: my night-dog Lope, a pet lamb called Puff, a cat, my mother.

I've seen men die in bed. On the gallows. At the end of a knife. I never sleep well, no matter where I lay my head, because I've never laid my head down in safety. My father used to come home drunk and wake me with blows. On the ship there were always thieves and mollies prowling about. Here, in this place, I've heard tales of what the blacks have done to shepherds at night.

The watch-box is small and draughty and rank. It's cold in winter and stifling in summer, but no worse than any other resting place.

I don't think I've slept easy since I was in my mother's womb.

⧻

I'm boiling water when Joe gets up.

'There's a blood trail,' I tell him. 'I should look for that wild dog or it might come back.'

Joe grunts, as usual. I've spent months in his company and know as little about him now as I did when we first met. He's a thief from Lambeth, doing seven years. His wife is dead. He likes cooking.

I thought once that Joe was quiet because of Carver. It wasn't wise to speak in Carver's presence. But Carver has been gone for three weeks and Joe still doesn't talk.

Not that I mind. I don't like Joe. We're here to do a job of work and survive as best we can. For friendship I have Gyp and Pedlar.

'I'll need the gun,' I say. 'For the wild dog.'

Joe hunches his shoulders. 'You'll come back after and tend to things,' he growls. 'I'll be over-busy, else.'

By 'things' he means the sheepfold, the woodpile, the washing and the cooking. I've no cause to argue so I dip my stale damper into my tea and chew, gazing at the hearth— which doesn't draw well, though it's lined with good stone. Not that sulky fires trouble me, any more than smoky huts do. I take no offence at dirt floors, wobbly stools or creaky beds made of canvas lashed to wooden frames. Some folk have no beds. No tea. No fires. I rarely had 'em myself, when I was young. A one-roomed hut is riches when it sleeps only two men. Tea is riches when there's sugar to sweeten it.

Now that Carver is gone, I'm able to find joy in these things. I still don't feel safe, though.

When the tea is drunk and the damper ate, I take the musket outside, where Gyp is waiting for me. Pedlar is trying to dig a hole under the wall. The hut is barred to both of 'em on Joe's orders, so Pedlar will always start digging whenever he smells food. I've filled a lot of holes lately.

'Pedlar! Gerrout.'

The mongrel slinks away with a sidelong glance that's a provocation. He has an ungovernable streak. My sensible Gyp, too dignified to scrabble in the dirt for a mouthful of mutton, comes trotting after me when I click my tongue.

We head for the blood trail.

The hut stands in a clearing full of tree-stumps. Beyond this grassy stretch a fence of thick forest lies in every direction, rising towards the south. A cart track passes through the clearing at its western end. The blood trail leads towards the brook beyond the eastern tree-line.

Gyp soon overtakes me, weaving and sniffing and skirting two headboards rammed into the ground. Though I haven't enough book-learning to read the names on 'em, I know which is which. The one on the left says 'Sam Jenkins'. The one on the right says 'Walter Hogg'. I never met either man but I know how they died. Carver told me. He enjoyed telling me.

The trail stops at the brook, which is stony and sluggish, its banks churned up by sheep. There's a mess of tracks in the mud and I'm casting about for fresh ones when Gyp yelps at me from the far bank. She's prowling around a gap in the undergrowth—the entrance to an animal pad, formed by the passage of roaming beasts. A spot of blood stains the ground nearby.

'Good girl.' Ah, but she's my treasure. '*Good* girl.'

All along the narrow path, a line of dark red drops leads us through an overgrown gully, a thicket of thorns and a stand of gum trees until it reaches the base of a rocky slope. I halt, wondering whether to go up or around.

Gyp knows. She heads uphill, her plumy tail waving. As we climb, the blood spots become smaller. By the time I gain the top of the slope, they're gone and Gyp is trotting in circles, whining softly. She's lost the trail.

I peer into the clefts between giant boulders cast about like builder's rubble, but there's nothing. Nothing on the hard, dry ground. Nothing on the grass stalks. The blood-stain I find on one patch of stone is dusty and faded and left by something much taller than a dog.

I unsling the gun and scan the silent bush. The sky is grey. The air is still.

There are blacks about; I know it. On my way up the hill I saw holes in the ground that weren't dug by native badgers. The blacks in this country eat orchid roots; sometimes they dig around the base of trees. Joe claims they'll eat anything: grubs, shit, each other. He has nothing good to say about the blacks.

Gyp barks, high-pitched and urgent. She's yards away, tucked behind an outcrop of boulders that's crowned with scrub.

'I'm coming.' And quickly, too, with many a backward look. I don't like it here. This is close to where it happened. At the foot of this very hill, on the eastern side, is the place where I last saw Carver.

Now he's gone; perhaps he crawled away to die. I hope so. I pray so.

Planted at one end of a fallen tree, Gyp is barking at its great root-ball, her hackles raised. One hiss from me and she falls silent. The log is hollow. Blood spots and paw-prints lead straight into its black heart.

Gyp watches me, panting. I hunker down and see only darkness inside the log. But I know the wild dog is there. I can feel it.

Good.

The wind is blowing from the south, straight into the root ball. I have a tin of Lucifer matches in my pocket, and there's no shortage of kindling hereabouts: sticks and twigs and strips of bark. I gather up a handful while Gyp guards the log. She looks surprised when I drop my bundle onto the dirt beside her. But her ears prick and her eyes brighten as I make a noise like a match being struck. She bounds away, wagging her tail.

I collect more wood. There's no movement inside the log; the silence stretches out, taut as a bat's wing. I'm about to toss another load of kindling onto the heap when Gyp returns— with a stick so big that she has to drag it along behind her.

She adds it to my pile, then sits back and waits.

'Gyp! Come bye!' The command sends her streaking to the other end of the log. A sharp 'There!' makes her freeze. Her eyes don't move from the hole in front of her even when I scrape a match across sandpaper half a dozen times.

At last the head flares and I touch it to a sprig of dry grass. A wisp of smoke, a lick of flame and the fire is burning. I don't stay to watch the smoke blow into the root ball but go and stand by Gyp, aiming my gun at the log's rear exit.

Now we must wait. And wait. Smoke seeps through cracks in the wood. A lizard scuttles into the sunlight. Something cracks.

Suddenly—*boom!*—the wild dog erupts out of the root ball and dashes through the fire, scattering sparks. Gyp races after it. 'Gyp! No!' I can't risk a shot or I might hit her…

Dammit.

⊬

In Ixworth I used to trap eels. I would drop a noose around the mouth of a muddy burrow then wait by the water, still as stone, until the eel thrust its head out. If I was quick and the noose was smooth I could have an eel on the bank with one pull. It took a deal of patience, a stretch of clear water and a good length of copper wire.

There's no copper wire here. Even if there was, I'd be hard put to snare a wild dog in a noose. An eel can't smell you but a dog can.

I don't know who owns the eels in this country. The King, no doubt. He owns 'em all, back home, though my father wouldn't have it so. My father used to argue that poaching wasn't theft because wild animals were gifts from God. No matter how much common land a gentleman might have enclosed, there wasn't a single partridge in all of England that truly belonged to him, so my father said.

Some of the farmers near Ixworth had bills posted once, forbidding the collection of mushrooms and bilberries on their land. My father tore down every bill he could find and used them as spills to light candles. He hated being told what to do.

He wouldn't have lasted long in New South Wales.

⧢

I can't find that dog.

Perhaps he went to ground in a badger's burrow. The brown badgers here dig burrows bigger than anything I've seen at home—burrows that would fit a nursing sow with ease. I've heard that the blacks send their youngsters down these burrows to hunt, though I'm not sure if it's true.

I once saw the chamber inside a badger's burrow and it was easily as big as a watch-box. The blacks had dug down to it, I'd guess, since the chamber had its own chimney. I'm sure a roast badger is well worth sinking a six-foot shaft for, even with tools made of shell and stone. Not that the blacks are ill-equipped. They can carve a weapon so finely balanced that it returns to you when you throw it.

One time Carver stole a woomerang that wouldn't come back to him. I doubt I could have done better even if he'd let me try, for it must take years to master. In the end he burned the thing.

Gyp is getting nowhere, roaming hither and thither, her nose skimming the dirt. Our quarry must be upwind. All I can smell is bush and native squirrel musk, and… What's that?

Corruption. The faintest whiff of corruption.

My throat tightens as I click my tongue, calling Gyp to heel. There's something dead hereabouts. It can't be too close or Gyp would have found it already but I'm scared now. Scared that it might be one of my sheep. Or worse—that I'm smelling Carver.

Is this where he died?

The stench isn't easy to follow; it comes and goes on the breeze. Crushed undergrowth releases a spicy scent that masks the stink of dead flesh. Suddenly the brush parts and I stumble into a small clearing that looks man-made with its cut wood, white ash, old fire-pit…

Who was here and when? Their tracks are long gone. They've left no midden. I'm casting about, looking for traces, when I catch the faint buzz.

Is it bees or flies? If it's flies, then I'm listening to the sound of death.

I follow the noise back into the bush, where I soon pass a marked tree. Someone has cut footholds into its trunk. The blacks do that; I've seen such trees before. One, I recall, had a hive in its branches—but there's no hive in this tree. The buzzing comes from somewhere else.

I stop to finger the lowest foothold, which isn't fresh. It looks days old. Weeks, perhaps. The blacks weren't here last night.

That will please Joe, who's even more frightened of 'em than he is of Carver. I don't know what to think. I've heard tales that would turn your stomach, but the signs I've found have never unnerved me. If the blacks eat each other, I've seen no hint of it. The worst I've seen is a bit of roasted snake skin, licked clean.

As my breath hits the trunk, something stirs there. It looks like animal fur, grey and very fine. Opossum fur? Perhaps someone climbed the tree to hunt an opossum.

'Gyp!' She's disappeared into the bush but comes quickly when she hears her name. Then she follows me towards the hum of massed insects, panting and grinning. She wouldn't be grinning if there was anything to fear.

There's a break in the trees again, where a great wedge of exposed rock slopes gently down to a shaggy thicket. At the base of this shallow cliff, one tree is engulfed by flies.

'God save us.' I know instantly what I'm looking at, though I've never seen one before. There's a platform resting in the tree with a man-sized bundle on it, sheathed in wood and bark.

That's a corpse, and it isn't Carver's. No black would have taken so much trouble with *him*.

If Carver perished hereabouts, he wouldn't have escaped the wild dogs.

⁜

I reach the hut at midday with nothing to show for my efforts but a scratch on one hand. Even Gyp is downcast. We've both been outwitted; somehow the wild dog escaped us. Perhaps it doubled back on its own scent.

Joe won't be pleased. I've wasted a whole morning.

As we hit cleared ground Gyp begins to bark and I look up from my boots, which need new soles.

There's a stranger sitting on the woodpile by the hut door.

His face is thin and scrubby; his brown curls are matted. His trousers are like mine—scattered with arrows—but his shirt is of red flannel. His wrists and ankles are like mine, too, marked by the scars of manacles and leg-irons.

'Don't shoot!' He has a thick Irish accent. 'I'm a friend— I'll not hurt ye!'

My gun's already half-cocked and aimed at his head. Squinting down the barrel, I can see he's no great age— a dozen years older than me at most. His beard is sparse. Patchy. He's all grime and sunburn.

'Don't shoot,' he says again. 'I'm sent by Mr Barrett.'

Mr Barrett owns the flock, the hut and the land they're on. All our supplies come from Mr Barrett. He sends a cart once a month from his homestead ten miles south.

He has five hundred head of sheep, three horses, two cows and half a dozen staff, most of 'em lags. He's been here five years and it shows. Though born a gentleman and book-learned, he's losing his quality.

His speech is as rough as his hands these days.

'He said you had a feller run off,' the stranger adds. 'Name o' Carver?'

Carver. God damn him. 'Yes.'

'Well—I'm yer new Carver.'

The last thing I want is a new Carver. But he knows the name and that reassures me. Slowly I lower my gun.

'Ssht!' I tell Gyp, who falls silent.

'I'm thinkin' you'll be Tom Clay.' The stranger grins. One of his teeth is missing; I wonder if he lost it to scurvy like me.

He nods at the dog and says, 'This'll be Gyp.' Then he looks at Gyp and jerks his head in my direction. 'Unless you're Tom Clay and he's Gyp?'

What a fool. Does he think he's funny?

'I'm Tom Clay.'

'And I'm Phelim Cavanagh, but you can call me Rowdy. Everyone does.' He gets up and strolls towards me as if he owns the place. 'So where's—ah—Joe, is it? Joe Humble?'

'Joe's with the sheep.' And won't like this cove one bit. Joe's not over-fond of the Irish. Or of jokes. Or of strangers.

Not that we see many strangers. It feels queer to be looking at a new face.

Rowdy's eyebrows climb his forehead. 'I thought Joe was hut-keeper?'

'He is.' I make an effort. 'But I had to chase a wild dog—'

'—and you're down a man,' Rowdy finishes with a nod. 'Did you kill it?'

I shake my head.

'Ah, well. Next time,' says Rowdy, brisk and bright. 'So what now? Cup o' tea?'

Tea. Curse the day. A wagon must have brought him and I missed it.

'Did you bring any?'

He seems puzzled. 'What?'

'Did Mr Barrett send tea in the wagon with you? Or sugar?' We need 'em both.

'No, but I brought meself,' he says, all jaunty and strutting. 'What else could you want?'

What else? Why, to go back to England. Barring that, I want my mother, my freedom, a house with windows, a horse, a dairy cow, some chickens, and plum pudding for dinner every day.

One thing I don't want is a strange lag poking about asking questions.

'We need to move the hurdles,' I tell him, and go to put the gun away.

2

BACK HOME, we couldn't afford brewer's yeast for the bread even when we could afford a kitchen. Sometimes Ma would make her own yeast with flour and water and hops. On winter nights she would take it into bed with her, to keep it warm.

When I was cold I had to sleep with the dogs. The yeast was more important.

+++

There's no yeast in damper—just flour and water and salt. The skill is all in the kneading and the baking. An hour's kneading goes into every good damper, and a foot of hot ash into every good bake. I can lay a fine baking fire and time it to perfection, but I can't knead like Joe, who has bigger hands with more strength in 'em.

I've been kneading for more than an hour and the dough still isn't smooth enough.

The fire crackles. The door stands open. Beside it, the woodpile is now almost as high as the eaves. Beyond the woodpile, the hurdles have vanished—there's just a big patch of trampled grass and sheep shit.

The new fold stands hard against the hut's back wall. It's all of a month since the sheep last grazed there, because it unsettles 'em to smell the wooden frame nearby. Joe calls this frame the gallows, though I think it looks more like a flogging triangle. We hang the carcasses on it to bleed out before skinning.

Mr Barrett doesn't grudge us fresh meat as long as we don't eat too much of it.

Moving the sheepfold took a long time because the ropes were so tightly knotted and Rowdy doesn't understand ropes. He's not a seaman. He's a city boy who's never worked with horses or on a farm. Raised in Dublin but gaoled in England, he came here a year ago, lagged on a seven-year stretch for passing counterfeit coin in a pub. I've learnt more about him in four hours than I've learnt about Joe in four months because Rowdy never stops talking. He talked while we moved the hurdles. He talked while we split and stacked the wood. Sometimes he asked questions: how many sheep in the flock? When would the next delivery come? What was I lagged for?

To shut him up, I sent him off to the creek for water, but

he's on his way back now. I see him out there, lurching and stumbling, a full bucket dragging down each arm.

The sun is low. The shadows are long. Joe will be returning soon.

'Mother o' God!' Rowdy staggers over the threshold and lets his two buckets drop to the floor. Then he collapses onto the nearest bed. 'Sure, but that was a weary walk,' he complains. 'Why is this hut not close to water?'

'The brook floods.'

'Oh.' He's silenced, but only for a moment. 'So…poor old Sam Jenkins, eh?'

What?

'I saw yer two headboards down by the brook,' he says. 'Sam Jenkins and Walter somebody…'

God ha' mercy. 'They're dead.'

'I should bloody well hope so.' Rowdy sits up. 'What happened?'

'Blacks.' I'm lying of course, but I don't trust him. I don't trust anyone.

Rowdy nods. 'Did they get you too?' He taps his own temple in the exact spot where Carver struck me with the musket. I hardly feel the scar now that the scab's gone.

'I fell,' is all I can think of to say. I don't think he believes me. When he looks at me sideways, I turn back to my kneading.

'You're doing that wrong, boy.' He jumps up, comes over and jostles me aside. Then he plunges his hands into the dough. 'See—you're treatin' it like a gentleman,' he explains. 'You've gotta *flog* the bastard. Harder you punch, sweeter it tastes.'

I've never met a man in this colony who didn't think he had the knack of good damper. But I'm not about to argue. If Rowdy wants to make the bread, he's welcome to it.

He pounds the dough enthusiastically, the way my father used to pound me. 'There,' he says. 'Now you try.'

I try. He shakes his head.

'Put yer back into it!' he exclaims. 'Look at the damn thing, layin' there like Lady Muck! Great big lazy white lump—don't you hate it? Don't you want to make it pay?'

I just look at him. 'No.'

'Well, there must be *someone* you hate. Someone you want to thrash.'

There's someone, right enough. Someone I wish I'd killed. It must be written all over my face, because Rowdy smiles crookedly and points at the dough, saying, 'Pretend that's him.'

Come to think of it, Obadiah Johnson's face was exactly like a lump of dough. The rest of him was like a bag of suet or a giant boil full of pus. He plagued the life out of every lag on the *Lord Lyndoch* because he was a thief without conscience and the most vicious bugger on board. I saw him steal tobacco from the mouth of a dying man. I saw him 'accidentally' scald five shipmates with hot tea. I heard him tormenting more boys than I can readily name, and only dodged his attentions myself (more or less) by giving up my ration of lemon juice while the ship's supply held out. After that, my scurvy kept him at bay. He had no taste for bleeding gums or purple spots.

Gyp barks, her warning yap pitched high over a distant chorus of bleats. I go outside to join her.

26

Across the clearing, sheep spill from the bush like a foamy tide. Pedlar steers them, yapping and nipping, while Joe flicks a cane above their heads.

'Come bye!' I tell Gyp.

She launches herself at the flock on an outrun. I head in the opposite direction, towards the new fold, where I pull one hurdle open. The first cluster of sheep approach—Skip, Daisy, Dancer, Moll. They veer away slightly when they smell the gallows, so I steer 'em back with a wave of my arms and a bark that sounds like Gyp's. There's a slight chill in the air, though the treetops are still touched with golden light. As the sheep flow past, the dogs dart about, casting and gathering.

Whenever I see sheep herded, I think: that was us, aboard the *Lord Lyndoch*. We were herded up on deck every morning to have buckets of water thrown at us. Herded to the monthly haircut, the weekly service and the almost daily spectacle of a flogging. Herded through the fumes of hot vinegar or chloride of lime, which the surgeon claimed would keep us healthy.

I don't know how chloride of lime could have helped us. Fools poach fish with chloride of lime; it poisons the water. My father scorned the practice.

'Who's that?' Joe demands. He glares at Rowdy, who's propped against the wall of the hut.

'Mr Barrett sent him.'

I scan the sea of woolly backs, noting scars, stains, brands, gaits, chipped ears, crooked noses...

'Where's Sweet-pea?'

'What?' says Joe.

'Sweet-pea. She's not here.'

Alarmed, Joe glances around. Some of the sheep are already inside the fold, pooling against the hurdles as the rest of the flock pour in after 'em. Gyp's tidying up the stragglers: Mabel, Pudding, Doris, Rose.

But no Sweet-pea.

'Ah, the devil!' Joe growls. Damn fool. He's forever mislaying stock. Sometimes I wonder if he can even count.

I've never lost a sheep. Never.

'Have ye named every one o' them beasts?' Rowdy inquires as I stamp past him. With a nod I plunge into the hut, grab the musket and scoop up some spare cartridges.

Outside, Rowdy's introducing himself. 'Joe Humble? I'm Rowdy Cavanagh.'

Joe grunts. 'You worked with sheep before?'

'Aye,' says Rowdy, then adds, 'well—I've cooked a few.'

Ha! Joe's not going to like that. Shouldering the loaded musket, I head back outside. Past the woodpile, past Rowdy, past Joe.

'That'll do!' I call to Gyp. She abandons the few sheep still trickling into the fold. Pedlar can handle 'em on his own.

'Check yer traps!' Joe advises me as I walk away, trying to blame me for his own carelessness.

'Sweet-pea wouldn't go near the traps.' You fool.

'*Check yer bloody traps,*' Joe says sharply.

I shrug. Behind me, Rowdy's talking again. 'How did a lad so young end up out here?' he asks Joe.

'He's from Suffolk.'

'Eh?'

'He's one o' the Suffolk Clays.' Pause. 'Best poachers in the county.'

Best? I think not. My pa was hanged for killing a game-keeper. My brother was shot by the same keeper. I was lagged for a brace of pheasants.

Seems to me there's no skill in getting caught.

+++

I once had a long-haired lurcher named Lope. He used to run hares into my nets. Whenever I had to lie in a pond for hours, waiting for the keepers to pass, he would lie beside me, up to his chin in water, not making a sound.

He was caught one night and lamed. A gamekeeper chopped off three of his paws. He was no use to us after that, so my father shot him, then beat me for his loss.

If I were one of Suffolk's best poachers, I wouldn't have failed Lope.

He still haunts my dreams.

+++

A narrow animal-pad runs between two walls of brush like a road between hedges. From where I'm standing I can just see, in the centre of this path, the carpet of dirt and dead leaves that conceals my empty dog-trap. A small log lies in front of the trap, but it might not be small enough. I want my quarry to leap over the log, not swerve around it.

We haven't much time; dusk is stealing in beneath the trees.

'See this?' I say to Gyp. 'Empty. I knew Sweet-pea wouldn't go near the traps.'

Gyp doesn't answer. She's staring up at me, her pink tongue flapping. We'll never find Sweet-pea at this rate—not with so much ground to cover.

Slowly I squat until my eyes are level with Gyp's and my arm is around her neck. Together we contemplate the trap.

'You'd spy that, wouldn't you? Eh?' Of course she would. And so would any wild dog older than a pup.

Look. Think. What would draw a dog's notice away from the ground? There must be something—something like a wrecker's lantern. In Cornwall the wreckers used to lure ships onto reefs at night by walking along the cliff-tops with their lanterns swinging. Ma told me that. She was Cornish. She had black hair and eyes, just like me; she said it was on account of the Barbary pirates who used to patrol the Cornish coast. She said we both came from pirate stock.

But she was swarthy. I'm pale, like my father. He was a redhead, with a flaming temper to match his hair.

Distraction. I need a distraction. Something high off the ground...

My shirt-tails are ragged from all the strips I've torn off 'em, but I need another piece. Not a big one. The cloth is so threadbare that a single rip suffices; I rub some grass against the rag and scrub the soles of both boots with the same grass, which I crunch between my hands until I'm coated in its rich scent.

'There,' I tell Gyp, so she won't follow me. One step forward. Two steps. Carefully skirting the trap, I stop just a few feet beyond it and grab a long, narrow branch. This branch is springy enough to arch over the pad and long enough to be fixed to a bush opposite.

Finally I knot my rag around the twig, in the very centre of the arch. It flutters like a white flower against the dull green bush.

Gyp studies it with interest.

'Not looking at the trap now, are you?' I join her again, dipping down to see what she sees. There's the pad. There's the log. And there's the rag, drawing my eyes away from the trap. If I were a dog, I wouldn't be watching the ground while I stepped over that log. My gaze would be travelling up, up, up…

Wait.

Gyp yaps as my muscles tense. Slowly I straighten my knees and stare at the eastern horizon.

Above the tree-line, in the distance, a faint wisp of smoke is drifting into the sky.

╫

The blacks carry their fire with 'em. A family once passed me in the forest and I smelled their smoke. There were a dozen at least—mostly women and children. They moved like shadows, falling silent when they saw my flock.

I thought to myself: I'm dead. But when I ran, they didn't chase me.

Later I saw the smoke of distant fires. Though I counted six columns of smoke, I knew by then that many fires don't always mean many blacks. According to Mr Barrett, the blacks will camp around a central fire and use other fire-pits to light up the bush and mislead their enemies. But this ploy has never confounded Mr Barrett's men, who are always mounted and who move so quickly from fire to fire that the blacks don't have time to escape. Mr Barrett is proud of that. He says he doesn't want his farm burnt down by the blacks and their fires.

I'm inclined to think that the blacks must fish with fire. I've found burnt faggots lying near waterways beside abandoned rods. There's nothing like a flaming tar brand to bring trout to the surface of a brook; I learned that at my father's knee. O' course, the spear I used to fish with was short and pronged, not taller than a man and barbed at the point.

But I was pleased to learn that the fish here behave much as the fish at home do. It's been of great use to me, knowing this.

You can get very tired of salt beef and fresh mutton.

‡

'Campfire!'

Joe looks up at the sound of my voice. He and Rowdy are already eating their supper: mutton, pickled cabbage and damper hot from the ashes. The smell of baking fills the hut; Pedlar's been trying to dig under the wall, and I have to push him aside as I enter.

The door slams shut in his face.

'Where?' asks Joe, through a mouthful of cabbage.

'Past the river. A long way.'

He grunts. I drop the musket and pounce on my rations, which are sitting in a tin pannikin by the fire.

'Did you find the ewe?' he says.

I shake my head. Joe mutters a curse.

'Mebbe the blacks took yer sheep.' Rowdy's tone is lively. 'Mebbe they're eatin' it now. Mebbe Tom saw their cookin' fire.'

Joe scowls. 'She ain't my sheep, she's Barrett's,' he says fiercely. 'And we could all be flogged if she ain't found.'

'Not me.' I'll take no blame for this. 'I didn't lose her.'

Joe lashes out, but he's not quick enough. I dodge the blow and Rowdy blocks the next one, for no reason I can see.

'Now then, gentleman,' he says. 'Birds in their little nests...'

'That bloody mongrel let it stray!' Joe snarls. "Tis the dog should be flogged!' First he blamed me for his mistake; now he's blaming Pedlar. But nobody's going to touch that dog. Not if I can help it.

'Could ye not say we ate the sheep ourselves?' Rowdy says. 'Better to run short o' mutton than risk a floggin'...'

Suddenly, in the distance, a wild dog howls. Another joins in, then another.

Outside, Gyp and Pedlar respond.

'Sounds like an Irish wake,' says Rowdy.

Joe stuffs the last of the mutton into his gob, grabs the gun and heads for the door, still chewing.

'Goin' to be a busy night, eh, Joe?' Rowdy calls after him.

Joe bangs the door shut behind him as he leaves. Rowdy waits for a few seconds before turning to me and saying, in a low voice, 'Was it him did that to ye?'

Again he touches his temple in the place where Carver struck me. I shake my head.

'Who did then?' he asks. 'And don't tell me ye fell, because I know ye didn't.'

He likes to pry, this one. A nosy man who talks too much. I'd be mad to trust him.

My mouth is full of meat, so I can keep mum without giving offence.

''Twasn't Gyp, I'm sure,' he continues. 'That dog's a gentleman.'

'She's a bitch.' Doddy-brain.

'Aye, but I've known many a lass to be a gentleman,' he replies breezily. He jumps to his feet and stretches. 'So how d'ye pass the time of an evenin'? Sing a few songs, do ye? Dance a few reels?'

Is he joking? He must be.

'I know! Private theatricals!'

He thinks he's funny. There's no cause to laugh at me and Joe just because we don't talk much. Rowdy would be holding his tongue as well if Carver was here.

'I'll feed the dogs,' I tell him, so he won't ask me where I'm going. 'You can wash the dishes.'

He throws me a salute but doesn't reply, thank God. My only fear is that he'll talk in his sleep. At first I was thankful he'd come to free me from the watch-box at night. I wanted to sleep in my own bed again with no duty to disturb my dreams.

Now I'm not so sure. If sleeping in the hut means sharing it with Rowdy, I may come to regret the watch-box.

Carver might have been a black-hearted villain, but at least he didn't talk all the time.

＋＋

My father trained me to silence the way he trained his dogs, with food and a cane. He trained me to be silent in the coverts, the hedgerows, the house, the court. Speech, he said, was poison. It scared the game, alerted the gamekeepers and betrayed your friends and family.

Dogs don't talk, and they're no worse for it.

The Bible says, 'He that keepeth his mouth keepeth his life: but he that openeth wide his lips shall have destruction.' Carver taught me the truth of this.

Rowdy Cavanagh is talking his way to disaster.

3

MY EYES snap open. The dogs are barking. The roof above me is barely visible in the lamplight.

Rowdy stirs in the next bed. Sitting up, I push off my sheepskin, pull on my boots and snatch up the burning lantern. Then I head for the door.

Gyp sounds frightened; I don't like this.

Outside, the clearing is awash with moonlight. Black stumps rear out of the silver grass like rotting hulks on a calm sea. Joe stands near the watch-box, squinting down the barrel of his musket, sweeping it back and forth, back and forth.

'Wild dogs?' I call to him.

'Dunno...'

Gyp falls silent when I hiss at her but Pedlar keeps sniffing and whining at something on the ground—something that gleams in the glow of my lantern.

I stoop to look.

God ha' mercy. 'Joe!'

'What?'

'This is meat, here.' Poisoned meat, no doubt. '*Cut* meat.'

'What?'

'Fresh mutton!' Tossed from a distance. 'Bait, Joe.'

'Who's there?' Joe shouts. Then another voice makes me jump.

'What's goin' on?'

Rowdy has appeared in the doorway of the hut, looking sleepy and ruffled. I'm about to answer him when the dogs erupt into a clamour of snarls and yips, straining forward, hackles bristling.

Someone—or something—emerges from behind a stump. Large and bent, hulking and misshapen, it limps out of the darkness towards us, silhouetted against the moonlit grass.

A *bear*?

'Jaysus!' croaks Rowdy and ducks back inside.

It's not a bear, it's a man—a man wearing a shaggy possum cloak. Soiled bandages trail along the ground behind one dragging leg. A makeshift patch covers his right eye. He's plastered with muck and missing two fingers. His head is like a block of rough-hewn wood, all sharp angles and old scars.

I recognise that broken nose. I recognise that mermaid tattoo.

I recognise Dan Carver.

'Stay back!' Joe aims the gun at him; I can see it shaking. 'Stay back, or I'll blow yer brains out, whoever you are!'

'Joe.' Are you blind? 'It's Dan Carver.'

Joe's jaw drops.

'Going to finish the job, eh, Joe?' Carver's voice puts ice in my guts. That low, level burr, calm and quiet even when he's about to kill you—even when you're about to kill him—that voice is like a pistol being cocked. 'You should have done it right in the first place,' he says.

'The way *you* would have?' I won't be cowed.

Carver's great head turns in my direction, his one eye glinting.

'I can't hurt no one no more,' he rumbles. 'I swear I'll stay mum if you do. Just give me food and I'll leave. For good.'

He advances one step.

'Don't move!' Joe's voice wobbles. So does the barrel of his gun. 'Stay back, or I'll shoot!'

Suddenly Rowdy bursts from the hut, brandishing a hatchet. That's when a shot rings out from the north.

Joe crumples and drops his gun. Gyp begins to bark as my lantern falls. Another shot splinters the door-jamb next to Rowdy and he darts back inside.

Two guns. I heard two guns out there.

Joe's writhing and crying on the ground, clutching his arm. Where's his musket? *Where's the damn—?*

I spot it just as Carver lunges. His limp's gone and I know I have to reach that gun first. He's pulling a duelling pistol from beneath his cloak when Pedlar bites his leg and he roars with pain. I grab the musket. Joe lurches to his feet and staggers past me towards the hut.

'Pedlar!' Let go of Carver or he'll shoot you. 'Pedlar!' I shriek. 'Come! Ped—'

Another gunshot. It's too late. Pedlar's on the ground, twitching and trembling, blood gushing from his head.

Pedlar. Oh, Pedlar. My poor boy.

'*Bastard!*' The musket seems to fire itself long before I take aim. I miss, of course, and now Gyp's trying to bring down Carver. 'Gyp, come! *Gyp!*'

She skitters back to me as another shot buries itself in the watch-box. Carver's still loading his pistol.

'Tom!' Rowdy screams. He's leaning out of the hut, pulling Joe inside. As Gyp slinks past them, Rowdy reaches out to grab me. He yanks me over the threshold and slams the door shut in Carver's face. Then he wedges the bar into its brackets.

Suddenly the door shakes from a heavy blow. Carver must be throwing himself against it.

Joe's on my bed, groaning. I can hardly see him through the tears in my eyes. Pedlar. Poor Pedlar.

Gyp whines and nuzzles my knee.

'Three guns!' Rowdy's voice is shrill. 'They've got *three guns!*'

He starts to pat the walls, feeling for chinks between the upright slabs. My own hands are shaking so much I can hardly reload. Tearing off the twist of paper was easy enough, but when I pour the powder into the priming pan, half of it spills onto the floor.

'Ain't no holes in them walls,' Joe tells Rowdy, through gasps of pain. 'We filled every one.'

'That won't keep him out, though, will it?' Rowdy retorts with a glare. 'Since he's clearly got a bone to pick.'

Damn. So he heard, then.

'We had to kill him or he would've killed us,' Joe blurts out. 'Same way he killed Sam, and Walter—'

'But ye didn't kill him, did ye?' Rowdy says. 'In case ye hadn't noticed.' The words have barely left his mouth when another voice cuts in from outside the hut. Carver's voice.

'I told you, Joe—you should've finished the job.'

Rowdy slaps his hand over his mouth, wide-eyed with horror because Carver's heard everything.

'You're right about them walls,' Carver continues. 'Sealed up tight as a drum.' After a pause he adds, 'We'll just have to find another way in.'

We?

God ha' mercy. He must have joined a gang of bush-rangers.

⊹

Carver never threatened me. He didn't need to. Instead he would talk about the things he'd already done.

He talked about killing three men in the hold of the *Mermaid* on the voyage out. He'd smashed the skull of one man and left him at the foot of a gangway so the death would look like a tragic fall. He'd thrown another man overboard so swiftly and silently that no one had missed him for hours. The third man's passing had been ruled natural when in truth Carver had smothered him because his coughing had kept the whole deck awake.

Carver also bragged about killing a black boy in the bush. He said he did it to clean up the 'vermin' on Mr Barrett's land. Said he shot the boy and stole his spear and woomerang, which he later used to kill Sam Jenkins and Walter Hogg. The blacks were blamed and a raid carried out, much to Carver's amusement.

He would hit me with the musket and the axe-handle. Once, because I wasn't gutting a sheep as he wanted, he jabbed the tip of his knife into my chest where the ribs meet. Another time, when the damper wasn't to his liking, he threw Joe onto the coals and held him there until his back was burnt.

Carver never said he was going to kill me but I knew he would. He hated that the dogs favoured me over him. He hated that I never lost a sheep. He hated that I could read tracks.

One afternoon he took me out to search for a stray sheep, but didn't bring the dogs with us. I knew exactly what was coming. So did Joe.

What else could we have done but save ourselves?

⁜

Carver crashes against the door again and again, trying to break his way in. The whole hut trembles.

'Here.' I seize Rowdy's bed and Rowdy dashes to help. Together we shove and drag it across the room until it's rammed against the door.

I wish it were heavier.

The only light is from the embers in the fireplace. Our only weapons are the hatchet, the musket and the knives. The axe is outside by the woodpile. We have food. Ammunition. Two buckets of water…

Suddenly Gyp erupts, barking wildly at a patch of roof high above her. There's a knife-blade stabbing through the bark overhead.

Someone must have climbed onto the woodpile.

'You're the one I'll start with, Joe,' Carver croons. He's still behind the door. So who's on top of the woodpile, chopping a hole in the roof with his knife?

'I'll string you up like a dead sheep,' Carver adds quietly, 'and lay yer guts open.'

A shattering impact shakes the whole hut. God help us, he's got the axe. He's trying to hack the door to pieces.

'Then I'll leave you to the wild dogs,' he finishes, 'the way you left me.'

Rowdy grabs a stool and shoves it under the widening hole in the roof as shreds of bark flutter down onto his head.

I raise my loaded musket.

'Listen, Carver—take them sheep,' Joe rasps. He lurches to his feet, staggers across the room and plasters himself against the wall by the door. There's a knife in his hand. The other arm hangs limp, dripping blood.

I can't worry about him, though. I have to watch the roof.

'They'll flog us,' he croaks at Carver, 'but they'll not blame you. We'll not say a word, I swear.'

The door splinters beneath another blow of the axe. 'D'you take me for a fool, Joe?' Carver sounds amused.

With a sudden flash of steel the knife above us vanishes. The muzzle of a carbine appears in its place. Rowdy's stool is directly beneath it. He looks up, grabs the muzzle and tugs it sharply downwards. It discharges into the floor.

A shocked Rowdy tumbles off his stool, still clutching the gun, and abruptly disarms Carver's friend. Two empty hands grope around overhead. For an instant I have a clear view of their owner's face framed in the ragged hole. His balding skull looks like a potato, brown and lumpy and crusted with dirt. His small eyes are set askew.

He jerks back as I fire. There's a sharp cry and a heavy thud.

'For Chrissake!' says Carver. The hacking blows stop; I can hear footsteps outside.

'Did you hit him?' Rowdy whispers, still cradling the captured carbine.

'How should I know?' I toss him a cartridge, then frantically tear at another with my teeth. Powder. Ball. Ramrod. I need to be quick.

'You're a damn fool, Nobby.' Carver's voice is muffled. 'Get up. *Now.*'

So I didn't hit his friend after all. Or perhaps I did, but only winged him.

'We ain't outgunned no more, Carver!' Joe exclaims. He's propped himself against Rowdy's bed, looking pale and sweaty and sick. If Carver's listening, he gives no sign of it.

By this time my musket's fully loaded. Rowdy is still fumbling with his own cartridge, so I reach for a dishcloth, toss it at Joe and say, 'Bandage.'

He needs to tie up that wound.

'You do it,' Rowdy murmurs. 'Is there no rum we can give him?'

Of course there's no rum. Why would there be rum? But Rowdy's right: Joe can't tie a knot one-handed. I cross the room and snatch away the half-folded cloth, which I tighten around the wound in his arm. He grunts in pain; I've a notion the ball's still in there.

Gyp hasn't stopped barking. When I hush her she whines, so I turn to see what's amiss and—

'Oh Christ,' says Rowdy.

Smoke is seeping through the roof.

'Water! Quick!' I head for the buckets but Rowdy gets there first. He picks one up and empties it onto the smouldering bark. There's a hiss followed by a billowing cloud of steam and he falls back, coughing.

Is Carver using the lantern I dropped out there? The eaves aren't so high; you could set them alight without a ladder or even a woodpile. And then you'd just have to sit back and wait, until the people inside were forced to bolt...

We can't leave through the door now that Carver's there with his axe and his pistol and his gang of bushrangers. There's no window. As for the roof—yes, the roof is on fire. Over in one corner, beams are beginning to blacken. Tendrils of smoke ooze past rivulets of flame.

'Look!' I cry.

Rowdy whips around, then grabs the second bucket and douses the fire above him. That's the last of the water.

We have to get out before we roast.

'Cockeye!' Beyond the door, Carver raises his voice.

'You guard the rear.'

God ha' mercy, we're surrounded.

Gyp has stopped barking; she's pressed up against me, her eyes on my face. Pedlar's absence is like a stab-wound. Poor Pedlar.

Pedlar.

'What the hell are ye doin'?' Rowdy whispers as I drop to my knees beside the back wall. Gyp joins me. I don't have to say a word; she's soon scrabbling away at the hole Pedlar dug there last week, while I scoop out the loose dirt that I packed in myself to block his passage.

'Tom?' says Rowdy, drawing closer.

'Quiet.'

Obediently Rowdy lowers his voice. 'What are ye doin'?'

'The flock's out there,' I hiss back. 'And bush on the other side of it.'

'Aye, but—'

'Help me.' We don't have much time. The fire's taken hold behind us, over near the chimney. There's smoke pouring in. 'Dig. Quick.'

Rowdy lays down his carbine and digs. Joe is coughing. He heaves himself off Rowdy's bed and stumbles towards us, reeling like a drunkard. When he finally reaches the back wall, he has to lean against it to stay upright.

'But I'll never fit through that,' he protests.

'Shh!' Rowdy flaps a hand, frantically trying to silence him.

'This isn't for you,' I explain quietly. 'This is for me.'

4

I USED to catch rats aboard the *Lord Lyndoch*. There was a plague of 'em, and the desperate crew plucked me from the hold and gave me the run of the ship. That included the galley. I doubt I would have lived else.

Ship's rats are canny, but no cannier than a fox. The trick to rats is patience—patience and damp sawdust. The crew had been leaving their scent on the traps and wondering why the rats fought shy. I had to explain that the smell of damp sawdust will mask any other.

One day I went down to the bilge, where we often left fresh water to keep the beasts below decks. Sure enough, when they saw my light, a good four dozen rats slipped away into the dark, save for one that was cornered. I had him backed up and glaring until he turned and disappeared, squeezing through a crack no wider than a nail-head.

The hole I've just dug makes me feel like that rat.

+

There are two sheepskins inside the hut. When I toss the smaller one over Gyp's back, the woolly sides of it drag in the dirt. So I tie the fleece around her belly with tarred twine.

Beside me Joe and Rowdy are quarrelling in furious whispers.

'Even if there *is* a man by the fold, he'll be lookin' at the roof,' Rowdy says, his face a mask of sweat. 'And 'twill be dark, besides...'

'Dark!' Joe points at the flames licking along the beams overhead, which are barely visible through a pall of smoke. 'We've a bloody great torch above us, jinglebrain.'

'Aye, but the sheep'll give Tom cover,' Rowdy begins, then erupts into a coughing fit.

Carver's bound to hear that. He'll wonder what we're doing by the back wall.

'Go!' I point across the room, trying to smother my own coughs. I'm already wearing the larger sheepskin tied to my waist and shoulders. 'Don't start out till you hear me. Wait for my signal.'

'Aye, if we've time enough,' Rowdy murmurs, glancing uneasily at the roof.

'Here...' Joe's eyeing Gyp. 'You're not taking the dog?'

What? Of course I'm taking the dog.

'*We'll* need it,' Joe growls.

I open my mouth, but Rowdy speaks first. 'We've got the guns, Joe. Tom should take the dog,' he says softly, then jerks his chin at the door. 'Come and we'll move that bed,' he adds as a whirl of embers fills the air behind him.

Joe grunts. He's still leaning against the wall, white as salt. 'Don't you run off,' he warns me. 'You'll be needing our guns.'

I daresay he'd run off himself, given the chance. That's why he doesn't trust me. But I nod and he staggers after Rowdy, who's already shifting the bed away from the door.

When Joe tries to lift his end, one-handed, the weight is too much for him. He totters and nearly falls. His cough makes me wince; Carver will hear that too.

Rowdy motions for Joe to unbar the door while I fill my pockets with cartridges and tuck my sheathed knife into my waistband. The hilt digs into my belly as I lie down on the dirt floor. In front of me the narrow hole dips beneath the wooden ground-plate before rising again. The sheep are just beyond it; I can hear their weak, wavering cries.

Pray God I'm not trampled.

A spark lands on my hand; it feels like a pin-prick. Gyp whines in my ear. Flat as a snake, wriggling like a worm, I inch forward into the hole, head cocked sideways, cheek pressed into damp earth, ear scraping against wood. Dust shoots up my nostrils, but I can't sneeze or cough in case Carver hears me. The sheepskin catches on the ground-plate and I grope to free myself. Finally my squirming delivers me, grimy and gasping, into the sheepfold. I'm confronted by a forest of stamping, milling, churning hooves.

A blackened ember flutters down.

The sheep bleat as firelight flickers on their backs. They're frightened—of me, of the fire, of Gyp most of all. She's squeezing through the hole behind me now, also wearing a woolly white bonnet and coat.

Joe was right; the roof is as bright as a torch. I can see much more than I'd like to. Raising my head, I catch a glimpse of someone standing just beyond the southern fence. I don't recognise him. He's not the potato-face I shot at—the one Carver called Nobby. This is a rangy ferret of a man with a wall eye, a beaky nose and lank, pale hair that hangs to his shoulders. He's wearing a lacy neckerchief, a white linen shirt, a watered silk waistcoat and a Wellington hat, but he's no gentleman. His Adam's apple sticks out like a knee.

He's carrying a musket.

This must be Cockeye, come to guard the rear of the hut. He's looking at the roof, not at me, but I'm not taking any chances. I duck down and daren't lift my head again, for all it's draped in sheepskin and level with the beasts around me. I can't risk being spotted.

With my gaze to the ground I start shuffling on my hands and knees straight across the fold towards the western fence, which is close to the bush. There can't be more than twenty yards of cleared land between one and the other. In front of me, the sheep part like water before a ship's prow. Behind me, they bray in alarm; I don't know whether Gyp's frightened 'em or if they're scared of the fire. *I'm* scared of the fire. Embers are drifting down onto our backs. There's a smell of scorched wool.

'Carver!' Cockeye's shout is thin and squeaky. 'Do we want roast mutton, or should I let 'em loose?'

From the front of the hut Carvers calls, 'Wait,' his voice almost drowned by the clamour of sheep. There's a scuffle behind me as some of them jerk out of Gyp's way. I hope they're not running from her. Surely they've not enough room to run?

This fold is a close fit. I was counting on it. I don't want Cockeye spotting any suspicious breaks in the carpet of sheep's backs.

'Dammit,' says Cockeye. Why? Has he seen me? A sheep's piercing scream cuts across a chorus of frantic bleats. It might have been Pudding but I can't check. All I can do is crawl, eyes on the dirt, head tucked down.

'Carver!' Cockeye sounds worried. 'They're startin' to burn.'

'All right,' Carver yells back. 'Let 'em loose.'

What's happening now? Which hurdle will Cockeye open? His footsteps are drowned by the crackling fire, the crying sheep and the pounding of my heart. I need one look. Just one. A quick glance, is all.

And there he is at the sou'western corner of the fold. He's trying to untie the ropes one-handed. (Good luck to him; any knots of mine will be tight as caulking.) I wish he'd stayed on the southern side, but I've a notion this may still work in my favour. If he's trying to undo my knots, he won't be watching the sheep.

'Ach, you bastard!' he curses. I'm close to the fence, now; should I wait or go? Wait, I think. Cockeye's much too close to the western side. Perhaps I should head for the northern fence, well away from him. But can I risk the big expanse of open ground over there between fold and forest?

Gyp is sniffing at my ankles. Queenie and Piglet are jostling me. The crackle of the fire is getting louder and louder. I can feel the heat now; sweat's pouring down my face. The fleece on my back is warming up.

A sudden ripple of movement in the flock spreads outwards from the sou'western corner. Cockeye shouts and all at once I'm caught up in a stampede. Sheep surge past me. One of 'em jack-knifes away from Gyp, whose teeth snap as she guards my rear. This is it. Cockeye's opened the hurdle. We have to go.

'Gorn!' he yells and fires his musket. The flock reacts as one, flinching and pushing forward, all raised heads and rolling eyes.

'Cockeye?' Carver bellows. 'What's amiss?'

'Just moving the sheep out.'

That's Princess bleating; I know the catch in her voice. Tally treads on my hand. Bodies press against me. Together we're swept along, heading for the hole in the fence.

Where's Cockeye?

There he is, edging away from the flow of sheep and moving towards the hut. He's not looking over here; his gaze is on the roof. I'm close enough to see firelight flicker in his eyes.

Here's the fence, but the flock is speeding up and I'm not quick enough, not on my hands and knees. I'm falling behind. Gyp is beside me, now. Her fleece is slipping off her head but there's nothing I can do about that. Lifting my knees, I start to hop along on my haunches like a rabbit, praying Cockeye doesn't notice. He shouldn't. All I can see is bounding rumps as sheep spill through the gate and scatter across the clearing. Some have wisps of smoke rising from their backs. Some are heading straight for the bush.

That's where I want to go. *Faster, Tom.* I daren't look back. *Twenty yards…ten yards…five…*

Gyp darts ahead of me into the scrub. Some of the sheep wheel around when they hit the thick, leafy wall, but I keep going, thorns tearing my fleece, branches clawing my face. Relief surges through me as I reach cover.

++

Gyp is my fourth dog. I met her when I arrived at Mr Barrett's. He kept me on the farm for six months before he sent me out to the hut to replace Sam Jenkins. By then I was fast friends with Gyp, so Mr Barrett let her come with me. He thought she might help defend his shepherds from the blacks. He didn't know that Sam had been killed by Carver.

No one did.

On the farm Gyp was one of six dogs but at the hut the only dog was Pedlar until Gyp arrived. He was a shepherds' dog, assigned to the hut just as I was, and he'd served many different masters. That made him unbiddable, but all he needed was fondness and a firm hand. Carver would have ruined him if I hadn't come, so I'm glad I did. Despite everything, I'm glad I did.

Pedlar. He had a heart of gold to match his yellow coat.

He died defending me. I'll never forget that.

The blazing roof of the hut lights my way. The crackle and roar of the flames helps me too; it drowns the noise I make as I crash through the undergrowth. But I don't have much time. If the roof collapses, Joe and Rowdy are doomed. They'll either burn to death or Carver will pick 'em off when they try to escape.

Carver is visible now, because at last I'm facing the northern wall of the hut. He's stationed by the door with his back to me. Nobby stands opposite, clutching our axe, while Carver nurses the pistol. Blood is streaming down Nobby's face from a cut on his brow. Either my musket-ball grazed him or he was hit by a flying splinter.

He and Carver are waiting for Rowdy and Joe—and for me, of course, because they don't know I'm outside, creeping through the bush. But I can't do a thing yet. I'll have to keep circling. Both of 'em need to look away from the door, and that won't happen if I'm over here. The door faces east, so that's where I should be. On the eastern side of the clearing.

Pray God I reach the right spot before the roof comes down.

I wince at the sound of my own footsteps, even though Carver surely can't hear me through the snap and sizzle of the fire. Gyp pads along beside me like a ghost, her sheep-skin snagging on twigs and rough bark. Every time she jerks free, the sheepskin slips a little more. It unfolds under her belly and drags along behind her like a bridal train.

Something rustles in the bush, moving away from me. A possum? It sounded too big for a possum. God grant it wasn't a black. That fire could easily have drawn every black within miles.

I pause and peer into the shadows, my heart in my mouth. But the darkness is too dense. I can't see a thing so I move on as swiftly as I can.

Now I've a clear view of the door, and Carver's profile beside it. The light from above doesn't flatter him. He must have lost that eye when Joe hit him on the head.

A wandering ewe trots across the clearing. That's Pickle. I hope she's not burnt.

Just a little bit further…Here. This is the place. I'm opposite the door. I'm well-screened. I'm not too close. In my singed sheepskin, I could easily be one of those stray sheep.

Suddenly a cloud of orange sparks shoots into the sky as a corner of the roof disintegrates. Carver grins.

It's time.

When I click my tongue at Gyp, she starts to howl. So do I. We moan and yowl like wild dogs. I learned the trick of it as a lure, months ago. Sometimes a wild dog will come to investigate if you call to him, but if he dodges you the first time, he'll not come again.

Carver's head snaps around. Nobby turns to look in the same direction—just as the door slams open and Joe bursts out. Rowdy's behind him. Joe has the musket. He opens fire at Nobby, who drops like a stone, but Carver is quick. His arm jerks up and he shoots Joe in the chest.

'No!'

No, no, *no*. Joe falls with a choked yell, dropping the musket. Rowdy aims at Carver and fires. It's a flash in the pan. Carver ducks anyway, giving Rowdy a split second to drive the butt of his carbine into Carver's skull. Carver topples. Rowdy bolts.

He's heading north. *No! This way—over here!* I'm on my feet, helpless. Then Cockeye charges around the sou'eastern corner of the hut, his musket raised. He fires at Rowdy, who dodges the ball, running hard, weaving between tree-stumps as he heads for the bush. Carver staggers to his feet and nearly trips over Joe...

Joe's dead. He's lying in a pool of blood. His eyes stare. His mouth gapes.

What should I do?

Carver points at Rowdy's retreating back. He speaks to Cockeye but I can't hear what he says. Cockeye nods, already biting the tail off a cartridge. As he shakes the powder into his priming pan, he heads after Rowdy, stepping straight over Nobby, his comrade, who's been shot in the neck.

Nobby's dead too. Is he? I don't know. Joe's dead for sure. But Rowdy's gone—he's reached the forest. If he has any sense, he'll reload and hide in there. An ambush might work. He should wait for Cockeye, shoot him, grab his musket and run.

The roof collapses with a crash and a swirl of sparks. Orange smoke billows into the starry sky. Carver is reloading his pistol. There's blood on his cheek from the butt of Rowdy's carbine. He spits the tail of his cartridge onto Joe's bloody chest. His hands are steady as he shakes powder into the barrel, adds the ball, tamps it down. Then he turns his head and fixes his gaze on me.

But he can't see me—there's scrub in the way.

He grins like a dog.

I don't wait to watch him pick up Joe's musket. *Time to go, Tom. Run, run, run.*

The bush is dark and grows darker with every step. My eyes are still adjusting, but Gyp can see. Gyp can smell. She swarms along in front of me, dodging tree trunks. Branches slash at my face. Snatch at my shirt.

I'm making too much noise.

'I ain't about to gut you, Tom Clay.' Carver's low voice drifts out of the darkness behind me. 'I think I'll cut yer throat and hang you like veal.'

Oh God, oh God. My sheepskin's falling off. *Faster, Tom, pick up the pace.* Gyp's way ahead of me and I stub my toe and my breathing's too loud and Carver's going to catch me. He's got two guns. I'm dead.

Suddenly the ground drops away and I'm rolling, tumbling, bouncing—down a slope, not a cliff—but branches break and stones clatter and I fetch up against a log, striking my head and hissing through clenched teeth because I mustn't groan. I mustn't cry. I mustn't make a sound.

Gyp sniffs at my hand, whimpering. One sharp gesture shuts her up; her eyes gleam in the moonlight. Where am I? In a clearing? Wait—is this a *hollow* log?

'Before I cut yer throat, Tom Clay, I'm going to take yer dog,' Carver calls. He's coming. He's close. 'I'm going to stick a pole through her arse and roast her like a pig on a spit.'

Gyp growls.

'*Ssst!*' This log is our only chance. I'm small and so is Gyp—but she baulks at the mouth of the damp, crumbling hole. 'Gorn!' I whisper. She looks at me sideways and slinks in, the sheepskin slithering behind her. She doesn't like this. There may be a snake inside.

If there is, she'll have to kill it.

Carver's smashing through the undergrowth, making so much noise that he probably misses the snap of the leafy branch I break off as I wriggle into the log, feet first. God ha' mercy, this is tight. Splinters prick. Gyp nudges me. I nudge her back.

The log is overhung with ferns and saplings and bushes that I call blackthorn, for want of a better name. None of the plants in this country seem to have names, except the timber. The little birds are nameless too—I have to name them myself, since no one else can tell me what they are.

Once inside the log, I leave the branch propped against its mouth to shield me. Carver's footsteps are drawing nearer.

'I'm going to find you, boy. I won't stop till I do,' he warns. He's close now.

I hold my breath. He's panting. I can hear the crunch of dry leaves under his feet. Golden light glints on the leaves in front of me, because he has our lantern. He smells sour. Somewhere an owl makes a booming noise.

He kicks the log.

I almost gasp. The light grows brighter and I shut my eyes tight, so they don't gleam.

Please, Gyp—please, Gyp—please don't growl.

A gun fires somewhere to the north.

'Got 'em,' says Carver, with relish, then raises his voice. '*Cockeye? Where are you?*' His footsteps move away. I can feel Gyp's breath on my calf.

He's leaving. But for how long?

If he thought I was here he wouldn't have left. He would have fired into the log. Perhaps I should stay instead of blundering about in the dark, getting lost. Getting hurt. Getting shot at.

Carver has a light. He has men and guns. All I have is Gyp.

I'm like a rabbit gone to ground. I need stealth, not courage.

My life depends on it.

5

WHEN DAN Carver tried to kill me he took me into the forest to look for a lost sheep. He'd already killed the sheep, of course. Her name was Gilly. He'd cut her throat and stuffed her under a low-hanging rock. Then he'd hidden his spear nearby.

We reached the place too quickly; it was clear that he knew where she was, for all his feigned surprise. He told me to drag her out but I didn't want to turn my back on him. He would have speared me the way he had Sam and Walter, then blamed the blacks. He would have said we'd gone our separate ways.

So I refused to touch poor Gilly.

He couldn't shoot me, because the blacks have no guns, but he hit me with the butt of his musket. Though I tried to run I was dazed from the blow; he would have killed me if Gyp hadn't come. She dashed out of the bush with Joe close behind. Joe used his axe before Carver could shoot, striking a mighty blow while Gyp was still worrying Carver's leg.

That first blow felled Carver; the next killed him, or so we thought. I kicked him and felt for a pulse—his neck was slick with blood. I was frightened and Joe looked as if he was going to faint. He was already winded because he'd never been much of a bushman. I doubt he would have found me without Gyp.

We lost our heads then. We thought we'd bury Carver and pretend he'd bolted, so we left him where he lay. I went to help Pedlar with the sheep. Joe went to fetch a shovel.

When he returned, Carver was gone. We didn't know if the blacks had taken him or if he'd fled on his own two feet.

That's why he's stalked my dreams ever since.

+++

I wake with a start, gasping. Carver's voice is still ringing round my skull; he was in my nightmare, roasting Gyp on a greenwood spit.

But Gyp is alive, her hot breath grazing my ankle. She whimpers as I squirm. A pale light is trickling into the log. Daybreak. It must be daybreak.

How long did I sleep? Too long. I'm parched and my belly is growling and I need to piss. Trouble is, I don't know where Carver might be, or if I should risk leaving the log. I can't stay here forever, though. And I'm a better bushman than

Carver, as long as I can see. Besides, the branch I pulled in front of the log is wilting. He might notice that, if he passes again. I would.

Slowly I push the branch aside, crawl out into the silvery dawn, rise, look around. The air is very still and smells faintly of smoke—not of blood or gunpowder or old sweat. In other words, it doesn't smell of Dan Carver.

I can see the smoke. There it is, drifting above the treetops into a cloudless sky. It must be coming from the hut, which is much too close. Gyp and I have to leave. We won't be safe until we reach Mr Barrett's homestead.

As I slide out of the log, Gyp wriggles after me, still dragging the sheepskin. She shakes herself. I put my ear to the ground, but can hear no distant pounding of feet. When Gyp nuzzles my armpit, I hug her.

'Shh,' I whisper. 'We must be very quiet...'

She understands; she always does. Her tail wags. Her sheepskin's falling off, but that's all right because I need it. Before I do anything else, I need to cut up that sheepskin.

I don't want much of it—just two small pieces, each big enough to fit over a boot-sole. If I turn the fleece towards the ground, it'll mask my footprints. Luckily I sharpened my knife yesterday: it slices through the leather without too much sawing or hacking. I can't use Gyp's tarred twine, though. The sheepskin has to stay on her back or she'll leave her hairs on twigs and thorns. Her tracks are fine—they could belong to any wild dog—but her black-and-white coat isn't common in this country. I want her to leave tufts of wool, like a lost sheep.

Instead of using Gyp's twine on my feet, I cut the cord that's been fastening my own sheepskin around my waist. Now I have a sheepskin cloak that hangs loose from my shoulders and two sheepskin boot-soles, which leave only the faintest, blurred tracks. My knife returns to its sheath. Gyp's sheepskin returns to her back. Then I take a quick piss and make for the cart track that leads all the way to Mr Barrett's homestead—and to his neighbour's farm as well, if I turn right instead of left, though that's fifty miles to the north; I can't get there on foot. Even Mr Barrett's house will be hard to reach before nightfall without a horse. That's why I need to hurry.

There's an animal pad heading west, so I follow that until it veers away to the south. Now I have to make my own path—and a lot of noise into the bargain.

An axe would help but the axe is back at the hut. I don't want to think about the hut. Or Joe. Or Pedlar. I need to concentrate on where I'm putting my feet. I need to keep my ears pricked and my eyes peeled, my head down and my arms up.

I crash through the bush, getting ripped to pieces. Gyp pads along ahead of me like a wraith. The branches that claw at my shoulders are too high for her. But she does have to skirt around a few tangles of brush and fallen timber. Once or twice she sniffs at a scent-trail.

Suddenly she barks.

I look up: Meg has wandered into the bush. She gives a plaintive bleat but I can't do anything for her.

'Sorry, Meg.' I really am sorry. Beyond her, a solid wall

of leaves blocks my route. As I push through it I wonder if I've made a mistake. Am I off course?

Finally the matted branches give way and I stumble out onto the road. There's no one on it; that's a relief. To the south, nothing. To the north, nothing—except a pile of fresh horse shit, gleaming and covered in flies. The hoof-prints scattered around it are fresh too.

Carver has horses.

I can't stay on this road.

'Come!' Gyp is making a beeline for the manure but returns when I call and pursues me back into the roadside scrub, where I pause for a moment to think. *Think, think, think.*

If Carver has horses, he'll use 'em. He'll keep to the road. But I don't have to.

I'll head for the hill, instead.

Since I've cut my own path through the undergrowth, retracing my steps isn't much of a challenge. It doesn't take me long to find the animal pad, which leads south towards the hill. I follow it past a fallen tree, through a patch of ferns, into a dry creek-bed and out again. Nothing I see concerns me. Bark's been stripped off one tree trunk, but the scar looks old and weathered. Dead leaves have been kicked up along the trail, but not by a man's foot; those are the tracks of a beast, though I'm not sure which kind. At home I knew every paw-print. Not here.

Sometimes I feel as if I'm half-blind, wandering around in ignorance. Mr Barrett showed me the native sassafras and the native red cedar because he cuts 'em for timber. Some of the other lags warned me against the nettle-tree, which stings. There are grass-trees and fern-trees and tea-trees (which can be used to make tea, though it's a harsh, bitter brew). But no one I've met can tell me what the red blossoms are that appear in the spring and turn into little nuts. No one can tell me what the native bears eat. No one can tell me which creatures leave the square droppings or the scribbles on the bark or the little tufts of grass surrounded by blue parrot-feathers.

At home I learned the forest lore from my father. In this place I've learnt almost everything by myself. I've learnt that white parrots squawk and red parrots pipe. I've learnt that snakes vanish in winter. I've learnt that the blacks strip off the white scales that appear on some plants—to eat, it seems, because I've seen tooth marks on discarded leaves.

I'm as lost in this place as I would be in the middle of London. I don't know what's dangerous and what isn't. The ants here bite like mastiffs. The leaves are sharp enough to draw blood. The very birds come swooping down to attack you.

Every step I take, the earth feels strange to me. I wish I had someone to teach me what I need to know. How can anyone live well in a place without knowing it?

Soon the path widens. The growth on either side of it thickens into a dense, green hedge. Gyp's nose is glued to the ground. I keep glancing over my shoulder, because I'm very, very anxious. This is a well-defined path. Carver might have found it.

Two birds swoop past, small and swift, the ones I call thorn-beaks. They look rattled.

I don't like this. We didn't scare 'em, so what did?

Gyp halts as soon as I click my tongue. Dropping to one knee, I press my ear against the dirt and hear a steady thumping. Before I can wonder what it means, something bursts through the green wall up ahead. I spring to my feet as a small kangaroo crosses the path, plunges back into the bush and is gone.

Gyp barks. Another kangaroo comes crashing out of the scrub, then another. The brush closes up behind them like a curtain. There are more on the way; that's the drumming of their feet I hear. They're fleeing something. Dogs? Blacks?

Carver?

Two more kangaroos sail past, flashing across the path behind me. They're frightened. The path ahead is straight and open for at least a hundred yards. If we're going to hide, we'll have to follow the kangaroos.

They don't like me chasing 'em. They certainly don't like Gyp. Bouncing away from us, they scatter through a thick wall of tea-tree and I have to shade my eyes to keep out the slapping branches. Gyp surges ahead. Then she barks, startled by a kangaroo that jumps right over her and keeps going.

'Shush!' Dammit, girl, there might be a man with a gun behind us.

If there is, I can't hear him through the noise of the kangaroos. Another goes by, then another. Gyp's keeping up with 'em, but I'm not finding it so easy. Even where the undergrowth has been flattened, I still have to push through the higher branches.

Wait. That's not kangaroos; that's something else.

A rhythmic stamping. Dry leaves crackling.

Footsteps. Someone's on my tail and Gyp's nowhere in sight.

I can't call to her. I have to stay mum. But the twigs snap and rustle when I pick up my pace. The thorns tug at my hair and my clothes, I'm stumbling forward, arms raised, head down, squinting, and all at once the ground drops away…

I hurtle out of the thicket. My feet slip from under me. My arse hits dirt and I'm sliding down a rocky slope held together by knots of exposed tree-roots. The canopy thins. Boulders rear up.

I don't stop until I hit one. The impact leaves me winded and Gyp hurries over, panting, worried. Her ears twitch. She hears the footsteps too: they're coming closer.

My knee hurts, but I've no time to waste on that. I signal to Gyp: a circling motion and a clenched fist. She darts off. Then I scramble behind the boulder, which is as big as a post-chaise. The ground around it is littered with rocks. I grab the largest, most jagged stone I can find.

All I can do now is wait. Poised to strike, trying not to pant, I crouch with my rock raised and listen hard.

Above me, at the top of the slope, the footsteps stop abruptly with a skidding noise, a rattle of falling pebbles, a sharp gasp, a familiar voice.

'Mother o' God!'

I don't believe it.

Rowdy Cavanagh teeters on the edge of the drop, carbine in hand, scratched and sweaty. He sees me and blinks.

'*Tom…?*'

Then Gyp hurls herself out of the bush and clamps her jaws around his wrist.

₊╫₊

I saw my first kangaroo on the way to Mr Barrett's farm. Though I'd heard tell of 'em, I hadn't believed such wild tales. I thought the old lags were toying with fresh meat. But when our rattling cart scattered half a dozen big grey beasts on the road and I saw 'em bob away like the bastard spawn of a deer and a rabbit—well, after that I was ready to believe anything I heard about this place.

Mr Barrett took me straight from the barracks muster in Sydney. I'd been two weeks on dry land in the barracks hospital, where I'd lost a couple of teeth to scurvy. But fresh food soon put me on my feet again and forced me out into the crowds that came as a great surprise, since I'd no notion that the town would be so hectic. After sharing a county gaol with one hundred and fifty souls, and the hold of the *Lord Lyndoch* with twice that, I'd hoped for more peace in this empty land. Ixworth is a small place surrounded by game reserves, so even Bury St Edmunds, where I went to trial, had come as a shock to me.

I'd hoped for a country assignment in New South Wales, and was given one by Mr Barrett.

He was looking for farm hands, but there were precious few on offer. Most of the other lags were city-bred—hawkers, navvies, shoe-binders, stay-makers—and not one of 'em knew a copse from a coppice. When Mr Barrett learned I'd been done for poaching, he asked me what game I favoured.

Then he asked me how I'd catch it. Then he told the overseer to loose me, and suddenly I was assigned.

Mr Barrett is a young man, but the harsh southern sun has scoured the bloom from his skin. He was born to a Cambridgeshire colonel, and was once an officer of the 17th Regiment. Perhaps that's why he deals out his discipline so roughly—or perhaps his temper has been soured by the fact that his wife is still in England. He drinks too much but never during the day. He's a magistrate and very free with the lash, handing out fifty for every theft as if he's lost patience with all the thieves in his employ.

I've seen a good number of Mr Barrett's men flogged, but never was myself because I don't steal. I have eyes in my head, so I don't have to. Though everybody at the farm picked the haws from Mr Barrett's hawthorn hedge, I was the only one with sense enough to eat the spring leaves. I was the only one who ever collected eggs from the birds' nests or noticed when the berries on a clump of flax disappeared overnight, after a party of blacks left footprints around it.

There's no need to steal food in a place where the bees don't sting and the eels clamp onto your dangling worm like a miser grasping a coin. At home, after my father was gaoled, I had to live on wood shamrock and pignuts half the time. So I've never been tempted to anger Mr Barrett by filching a handful of his sugar or a mouthful of his rum.

He's a hard master but not vicious. He trusts me with his dogs, his sheep and his gun. Sometimes he even speaks to me as if I have some sense, since he knows I'm a country lad who can pleach a hedge or set a snare.

I'd like him better if he weren't a fool. Only a fool would trust Dan Carver. Only a fool would believe Carver's lies. Mr Barrett thinks far too much of strong men, and Carver is strong. Mr Barrett is strong too, but Carver's stronger. He can carry a full-grown ewe under each arm and not get winded.

After Carver killed Walter Hogg, Sam Jenkins fled back to the farm and told Mr Barrett that Carver had confessed to the crime. Mr Barrett flogged Sam for absconding and insisted the blacks had killed Walter. 'Dan Carver's putting the fear of God into you,' he told Sam, 'so you'll not be so wayward.'

I heard this from Joe, who was there when Sam returned to the hut.

A few days later Sam was dead.

-++-

One word is enough to make Gyp stand down, but it's too late—she's already left her teeth-marks in Rowdy's arm.

She has good grip.

'I swear, I thought they'd got ye,' Rowdy mumbles. His colour is bad.

'Did you shoot Cockeye?'

He shakes his head. 'No cartridges.'

What a numbskull. His carbine is lying on the ground, so I pick it up and pull a cartridge from my pocket. Then I sit down beside him to load the gun while he tears a strip off his red flannel shirt and ties it around his wound—which is barely bleeding.

'They have our musket now,' he says.

They do.

'We need to get to Barrett's,' he adds, wincing as he tightens his bandage.

'Then where were *you* going?' I ask.

He stares at me. 'To Barrett's.'

I can't help but frown.

'South,' he says, pointing.

'That's not south.'

'It is.'

Reaching over, I pat a nearby tree trunk. 'Moss grows on the south side of trees,' I tell him.

Rowdy blinks as he absorbs this. He glances at Gyp, who's sitting nearby, smiling and panting.

'Well. I might have strayed,' he admits. 'But d'ye agree we should take the road south?'

I shake my head. 'Carver'll take the road. He's got horses.'

'He does not!'

'I've seen their traces.'

Rowdy looks aghast. He thinks for a moment, chewing his bottom lip. I poke a ramrod into the carbine's muzzle.

'That road goes both ways,' he says at last. 'Carver might not head for Barrett's.'

Have you lost your wits?

''Course he will.' You lobcock. 'He knows we've nowhere else to go.'

'But why risk it?' Rowdy argues. 'Why brave Barrett's guns just to revenge himself on us?'

'No witnesses.' That's Carver's watchword. He was lagged for highway robbery on the word of a living witness, and told me many times that he would never make the same mistake again. 'Carver knows we could hang him if we talk.'

Rowdy glares at me. 'Then it seems we're both finished,' he snaps. 'Since we can't outrun horses.'

'We can if we keep off the road.' Rowdy's carbine is loaded now; I wonder if he'll let me keep hold of it? 'That road is the long way to Mr Barrett's,' I say, because Rowdy's expression is blank. 'It goes halfway round the hill yonder. But if we go over the hill, we can warn Mr Barrett on the other side.'

In all truth, I'm not sure I want Rowdy with me on this trip. He's noisy. He's foolish. He's wearing a bright red shirt.

I know he won't leave without the gun, though. And I don't want him leaving with it.

'Ye can do that?' he asks. 'Ye can find yer way to Barrett's farm?'

I nod. The hill isn't high. Though long, it's level—a ridge more than a hill. I climbed it once to gauge the lay of the land.

'Well then, let's go.' Rowdy jumps up, holding out his hand for the carbine.

Again I shake my head. He's not going anywhere in those boots. 'Sit down,' I tell him, dropping the gun. Then I take out my knife and call Gyp over.

I need two more pieces of sheepskin.

6

GYP HAS saved my life three times. She did it when she attacked Carver the day he tried to kill me. She did it when she told me that there was a snake in my bed, and again when the chimney caught fire while I was asleep next to it. If she hadn't woken me, I would have burnt to death. So would Carver, though he wasn't grateful. He used to kick her whenever he could.

Gyp's ma was Mr Barrett's old collie, Scylla. She was a fine dog. I've never met Gyp's father, Bear, though I know he belongs to a man called Phelps, who visits Mr Barrett on occasion. Mrs Trumble, the overseer's wife, once told me Bear had saved a drowning child somewhere out west.

She also told me, more than once, that I was greedy, shifty, lazy and worthless. But she's the greedy one. Her husband's a lag—what she likes to call a 'government man'—yet she came here a free woman to be with him. So she thinks herself better than most and makes a great show of it, for all she's only Mr Barrett's cook. She eats more in a week than I do in a month, claiming all the choicest cuts and sweetest produce for herself.

Her husband would be flogging us bloody if Mr Barrett let him—I've not had a civil word from George Trumble. The others at the farm don't care for me either. Jim Percy is sullen and prone to fits of rage. Charlie McTeale finds his greatest pleasure in telling lies about people. When I first arrived at the farm, he claimed that I hadn't been lagged for poaching but for housebreaking. He said he knew me from the gaol at Bury St Edmunds.

It was a lie, of course. I was in that gaol for two months, awaiting the July Quarter Sessions, and I never once saw Charlie. He's not even a Suffolk man, though he says he was passing through. He's a horse thief himself but has no horse-manship; I refuse to believe he was an ostler, as he claims. I think he lied about that to win a place with Mr Barrett. He's certainly lied about the women he's bedded and the blacks he's killed, just as he lied by blaming me whenever he broke a crock or a tool. Sometimes George Trumble would believe him, sometimes not. I don't know who's taking the blame now that I'm off the farm. Jim Percy, perhaps—though Jim's not one to take ill treatment kindly. I once saw him chase after Trumble with a scythe.

Jim was flogged for that. I'm surprised he wasn't sent to Norfolk Island. Perhaps Trumble wanted the chance to torment him further; when Jim was still healing, Trumble would clap him on the back and set him to work in the sun so the sweat would sting his fresh scars.

Is it any wonder I've always preferred Gyp's company? She's not sullen, she never lies, and she doesn't fill your ears with endless, pointless, dangerous chatter.

⧾

Rowdy is so busy talking that he's blind to where he is. This is a well-used path, heading straight for water, but he doesn't comment on the musky smells, the droppings, the tracks, the feathers, the footprints, the marked tree trunks. When birds call and flit, he doesn't pause to watch them in case they're warning us of something bigger. When the wind shifts, he doesn't stop to listen for new sounds, or sniff for new smells. He just saunters along like a captain on a quarterdeck.

Why is he so careless? Because he's handsome? Because he's foolish? Because he has the gift of the gab? Has he never been beaten or robbed or betrayed? Has he never looked over his shoulder?

At least he's keeping his voice down.

'Was it Carver scarred yer face?' he asks.

I nod.

'Is that why ye tried to kill him?'

I shake my head. 'He tried to kill me.'

'Why didn't ye tell Barrett?'

'Because Mr Barrett wouldn't have believed us.'

74

'Why not?'

'Because Carver always used a spear.'

'A *spear*?' Rowdy seems puzzled. 'Where did he get that?'

'He stole it from a black he killed.'

'Oh.'

That's shut him up. I remember how scared I was when Carver first told me about the dead black. I remember wondering when the other blacks would descend on us to take their revenge. Carver had brought back the murdered boy's property; I felt sure that the other blacks would come for it. Aside from the notched spear and woomerang, there was a sharp flint, a finely woven basket and a net made of grey yarn spun from tightly twisted opossum fur. I spent a lot of time examining that net and it was a miracle of workmanship, as fine as anything I ever saw in a Suffolk trout stream at night—though I have to admit I'm not well acquainted with nets, since my father didn't favour 'em. They were too easily damaged, he said, by the weighted thorn bushes thrown into the dubs and pools to foil poachers like us.

The dead boy's basket impressed even Joe, who declared that it must have been stolen from a settler. Carver liked it too; he put his tobacco in it. But after he was gone Joe decided to burn the thing, lest it be used as proof against us. He burned the net, too. And the spear.

Carver also brought back an ear as a keepsake. He tried to dry it in the sun, but the ants consumed a sizeable portion. Later he took us to see the corpse and it was gone. Though Carver blamed wild dogs, I knew better. I had seen the fresh spike of a grass tree, chewed at the bottom. The blacks do that.

Gyp hasn't taken her nose from the ground in a very long time. There must be so many scent trails…even I can smell some of 'em. I've not walked this way before, but someone uses it a lot. There have been kids along here, drawing in the dirt. Dropping their plucked flowers. Spitting out tree gum.

Speaking of which…

'Christ. Who's that, now?' says Rowdy as I halt to peer up at the sky. Over to the sou'west there's a smudge of smoke.

Campfire.

'Blacks,' I tell Rowdy. But they're a long way off—too far to bother us. Gyp hasn't even raised her head.

'Are ye sure?' Rowdy asks.

Of course I'm not sure. But the footprints hereabouts are quite fresh. And even if Carver has gone, he wouldn't take his horses down that way. Why force 'em through the wilderness when there's a road nearby?

'How d'ye know they're blacks?' Rowdy says as I pass him.

'Footprints.'

'Footprints?'

I point at the ground. They're everywhere. I can't believe he hasn't seen 'em.

'Oh.' He pauses to study the marks. 'These are not Carver's, then?'

Carver's? Since when did Carver go barefoot, with a crowd of kids? 'No.'

'Bloodthirsty devils. They'll not be coming back, then? We'll not run into 'em?'

'Not any time soon. Not if that's their fire, yonder.'

'What if they're lyin' in wait for us?'

'You talk too much.'

It has to be said. The noise he makes in response is halfway between a snort and a gasp.

'If you talk too much,' I warn him, 'you won't hear what's coming.'

I can't see his face, because he's behind me. But when he answers, his tone is dry. 'We none of us heard what was comin', me lad, or we wouldn't be here now.'

That's true, I suppose. When I was caught with my brace of pheasants, the rain was teeming down, battering treetops, smacking against roofs, drumming on roads and making so much noise I couldn't hear the splashing of footsteps over the splashing of rain in the gutters and ponds. The keeper's hand was on my shoulder before I knew he was there.

Sometimes lately I've wondered if I did know he was there. I was so tired and cold and alone by then; when my father was taken there was no one left. The only welcome I received anywhere was at the beer shop he patronised— and the landlord there gave me a dry corner only because of the cheap game I brought him.

Perhaps I heard what was coming all too clearly. Perhaps I heard the silence stretching out before me and fled from it, straight into the arms of the law.

But I shan't say this to Rowdy Cavanagh. I shan't tell him that he should have learnt his lesson, or that the more he talks, the more likely it is Carver will hear him. Because if I do speak, he'll only answer. And then there will be more conversation.

As long as he's silent I can forget he's here—especially if I stay ahead of him. His voice bothers me. So does his face. Though his chin's like a chisel and his eyes are like corn-flowers, he still reminds me of Joe. They're part of the same picture. And I don't want to think about Joe. I don't want to think about what happened to him.

'Jaysus!' Rowdy squeaks as a distant gunshot cracks the air. I fling myself flat on my belly and he joins me a moment later. We both lie in the dirt, listening. At last I put my ear to the ground.

Nothing.

Gyp doesn't seem concerned. She shoots me an inquiring look, ears cocked. That shot was nowhere near us. There's no cause for alarm.

I scramble to my feet.

'What are ye doin'?' Rowdy whispers. He grabs my ankle. 'Stay down!'

'They're miles away.' To the nor'east, near the road; it may have been a misfire.

Even so, we shouldn't linger.

'If they're miles away,' Rowdy mumbles as I shake him off, 'what's the hurry?'

A stupid question, not worth answering.

'Tom?' He's following me, now, bent slightly at the waist as if he wants to keep his head down. 'What if 'twas Barrett's men shootin'? What if they've brought supplies up from the farm?'

'They're not due.' Here we are. Here's the river.

The rivers in this country are small and dry. This one is

more rock than water. It runs along the base of the hill, which rears up beside it like a great, sod wall. The white-limbed trees are clustered more thickly around the river than they are on the hillside. They're so thin on the crown of the hill that its jagged spine is clearly visible, even from way down here.

I can't see anything suspicious.

'Mother o' God!' Pebbles scatter as Rowdy pushes past me, following the trail to the edge of the river bank. He squats on a patch of sand and scoops up water to drink.

Doesn't the fool realise how exposed he is?

Gyp yelps. Sure enough, she's spotted something. But when I turn my head to look, there's no armed man nearby.

A stray ewe is standing in the water.

'Hello, Queenie.' Poor girl.

She bleats. Gyp cocks her ears.

'Queenie?' Rowdy says, splashing water on his face. 'That's a hell of a name for a sheep.'

Without bothering to reply, I head for the river. Gyp bounds ahead of me and wades into the nearest rill, where she starts lapping.

'Though now I come to look, she is the very spit o' the young queen,' Rowdy observes with a crooked grin.

What? 'She is not!'

'She is.' He points at Queenie. 'No chin. Pop eyes. And her nose is identical.'

Remembering the picture of Queen Victoria that hangs in Mr Barrett's parlour, I'm struck silent.

'This sheep's a deal more handsome, mind you,' Rowdy says, while I dunk my head in the water. It's good water: cold, clear, sweet, clean. I drink my fill and soak my shirt-tails and neckerchief.

'We've no time for a bite o' mutton, I daresay?' Rowdy's gaze is still fixed on the sheep. 'I'm a mite peckish, now my thirst is quenched.'

Is he joking? He must be. Else he's mad.

I'm about to tell him so when there's another shot—closer, this time.

Why do they keep firing when they must know we can hear?

⧺

My father was brought down by a dog.

The keeper he shot had a night-dog named Grumbo—a great bull mastiff, brindle-coloured so as to pass unnoticed in a moon-dappled wood. Like all keepers' night-dogs, he was trained not to savage his quarry but to hold it down until the keeper came. Grumbo's master was dead, however, so Grumbo kept my father pinned until dawn, when a passing farm-hand ran to fetch the parish constable.

This was on the Elveden estate. The keeper's name was Clegg, and he was the one who shot my brother. The constable and the underkeeper claimed that my father fought them and had to be subdued. I don't know the truth of this, but my father had lost use of his left hand long before he reached the Assizes.

He served as an example, I'm sure. Ixworth had long been known as a poaching village; there was much talk about the 'gangs' who set off to shoot pheasants from the

80

Mackerel's Eye. My father preferred to work alone, but it made no difference. Though he claimed that the shooting was accidental, caused by a dark night and a thick copse, he was sentenced to death.

Gamekeepers may 'accidentally' shoot folk, but not poachers. Besides, my father had threatened Clegg in the constable's hearing.

I never blamed Grumbo for what befell my father. Grumbo was a good dog who served a bad man. Grumbo didn't shoot my brother or hang fish-hooks on stretched lines at face-height, so that one of them took out my father's eye. Grumbo didn't cut off Lope's feet.

That night-dog knew to obey a call like an owl's hoot and was as silent in the coverts as ever Lope was. I heard that he once outfaced a young bull.

I wish him well, wherever he is. I've yet to meet a dog I would count as an enemy—save for the wild ones.

+++

Rowdy grabs a handful of my shirt. He begins to yank me across the river, splashing through puddles and stumbling on stones.

'Wait!' I dig in my heels, but he's stronger than he looks. 'This makes no sense,' I cry as I stagger after him.

Gyp follows us.

'Come on!' Rowdy's heading straight for the hill and I know why. The blacks' fire is downstream, the road is upstream and the gun is behind us; there are threats in every direction but one. We can't go back, so we must go up.

'What are they shooting at?' I demand, struggling to loose myself.

'At somethin' they think is us,' he replies. But he's wrong—I'm sure of it. Carver isn't so jumpy.

All the same, I can't stop Rowdy dragging me along until the steep terrain starts to wear on him. At last his pace slows and his breath quickens. When I finally wrench myself free, he lets me go without protest, happy not to be pulling my weight.

This is nonsense. I feel like a grouse being flushed. Why would they give us so much warning?

'Rowdy—'

'Shh!'

'Listen to me—'

Bang! Another shot.

Rowdy ducks. So do I, though I know the ball can't reach us. That gun is somewhere between the road and the river, about half a mile away—or perhaps a little less.

'Come on,' Rowdy says. He tries to grab me again but I stand my ground.

'Why are they firing?' I ask.

'To kill us, o' course.'

'No.' I shake my head. 'They're too far away.'

'Come on, boy!'

'Wait.' I've got it. They *are* flushing grouse. 'They're driving us.'

'What?'

'They're driving us like game.' I point to the west. 'We can't use the road.' I point to the east. 'We can't brave the blacks.'

I point uphill. 'They want us going straight up there—they knew we would.'

Rowdy stares at me. 'Don't be daft,' he finally says.

I turn away and start retracing my steps, moving downhill, where the trees are thicker. It all makes sense now. If I were Carver, scouring miles of forest for a man and a boy, I'd take my horse to the base of the hill and climb to the highest point. Then I'd herd my quarry towards my position by using the blacks to the east, the road to the west and an armed Cockeye to the north.

Carver's not on the road, he's on the hill. I'm sure of it. He's standing high on a crag, gazing down on the treetops like a hawk, looking for...what? A red shirt?

Pray God he doesn't have a spyglass.

'Tom!' Rowdy's reluctant to follow. He hesitates, even as Gyp lopes after me. 'Tom, wait!'

I'm not about to wait. Cockeye must be closing in. We'll have to be quick if we want to dodge him.

'Tom! Where are ye goin'?' He's chasing me, now; his footsteps tell me as much. 'For Chrissake, lad, I'm not a bloody poacher,' he pleads. 'What do I know about drivin' game? You don't need country ways to pass false coin—you just need to know how to talk to folk.'

Talk, talk, talk. That's all he ever does.

'How can I help you if I don't understand?' he continues breathlessly.

'*Shut your mouth.*' Numbskull. 'Do you understand that?'

He must, because he falls silent. Now I can listen for the tell-tale sounds of stalking: a whir of wings, the snap of a stick, the creak of leather. Gyp's listening too, as she sniffs the air. But she doesn't seem unduly concerned.

And here's Queenie again, wandering among the river rocks, pausing to shoot me a lost look. 'Sorry, girl,' I say, because we mustn't stop. Not for a moment.

Our one way out of this trap is the road. If Carver's up on the hill, it means he overtook us. If he overtook us, it means he was mounted. And if he was mounted, then his horse must be waiting at the western tip of the hill, where the road skirts its base.

We need to reach that horse before Cockeye reaches us...

Oh Christ. Musket shots. Two of 'em.

'Jaysus!' Rowdy freezes. He peers at the slope above him, trying to see where the shots came from. 'Two o' the buggers? I thought Nobby was dead.'

He was. I'm sure he was. 'Two guns don't mean two people,' I say. But if Carver's on the hilltop with two loaded muskets, why fire 'em both?

Wait. Of course.

'It was a signal.' Damn, damn, damn, he's warning Cockeye. 'He can see us.'

'How—'

'He's got a glass.' God knows how he came by it. I grab Rowdy and pull him into a patch of heavy shade. When I start to yank at his shirt, he slaps at my hands.

'What d'ye think you're—?'

'Come bye,' I tell Gyp. She dashes off to fetch Queenie. Then I look Rowdy square in the eye and say, 'This shirt is going to kill us. If you keep it, I'll leave you.'

84

'All right, calm down. No need to bounce me—'

'Give it here.'

As Rowdy peels off his shirt, Gyp pushes Queenie in my direction, flanking from side to side. Poor Queenie doesn't jib at this outrun. She's in distress, and happy to see a familiar face. Even Gyp doesn't fret her. She trots up to me like a pony, her heavy fleece bouncing. And she doesn't flinch when I drape the red shirt across her back, or when I tie the sleeves beneath her belly.

Good girl. That's a good girl.

I'd lend Rowdy my jacket, but it wouldn't fit him. He's too wide across the shoulders. And scarred, too, I see; a dozen lashes, by the look of it.

''Twas on board the *Hive*.' He catches my sidelong glance. 'I spoke out o' turn.'

And still he won't shut up.

'Here.' I shrug off my sheepskin cloak and pass it over. 'Put that on.'

'Ah, no.' He lifts his hand gracefully. 'I'll bide well enough till we reach the farm—'

'*Put it on*.' I'm not asking. 'We're safer as sheep.'

'Ah.' He nods then and does as he's bid. I struggle to fit Gyp's sheepskin across my own back, fumbling with the tarred knots while she watches intently. At last, with a word and a wave, I tell her to drive Queenie westward along the river-bed.

She's quick to respond.

'Well, now,' says Rowdy, gazing after the retreating ewe. 'That's clever.'

It is. If Carver's watching the red shirt, he'll think we're heading downstream. Perhaps.

'Come on.' I start moving in the opposite direction. A whistle brings Gyp back to me, though first she nips at Queenie's heels, to make sure that the ewe picks up her pace.

Poor Queenie. Poor girl; the blacks will eat her, I'm sure of it.

'So we're taking the road, then?' asks Rowdy—just as another shot rings out above us.

Rowdy flinches. I pause. Why only one shot?

Unless two means west and one means—

There it goes: the second shot. Two quick shots must mean 'they're heading west'. One shot, a break, then another tells Cockeye we've turned around.

Except we haven't. Queenie's the one who's trotting downstream.

I just hope she keeps going.

7

I'M WORRIED about the sheep. Queenie, Moll, Skip, Dancer…they're all out there, unprotected. They weren't made for this country. The wild dogs will hunt 'em. The blacks will eat 'em. They'll fall down holes and trap themselves in thickets.

They'll need me and I won't be there.

As a shepherd, it seems, I make a good poacher.

━┼━

'Was that a signal?' Rowdy wants to know. He's stumbling after me, hugging the tree line along the south side of the river. 'Are they watching Queenie now?'

I hope so, or we're dead. Gyp is padding along at my side, swift and silent. She knows better than to blab.

'Is there no one on the road, now?' Rowdy continues quietly. 'Is it safe for us?'

I wish he'd shut up. The river's gurgle masks the noise of our passage but he still shouldn't be talking.

'Would ye answer a question if yer dog asked it, I wonder?' Before I can do more than snort, Rowdy adds, 'Mebbe I should ask her. Gyp—can ye tell me where we might be goin'?'

Gyp doesn't reply so Rowdy speaks for her. 'Woof. Woof-woof-woof,' he says, then remarks in his own voice, 'Ah, well, now that's interestin'. And would you describe that as a tactical manoeuvre?'

God help us.

'Woof, woof. Woof-woof-woof.' He must think he's funny. 'I see,' he says. 'Thanks, Gyp, you've dainty manners. Not like some folk I could name—'

'Will you *shut your mouth*?' I round on him, furious. Doesn't he know what he's risking?

'Don't blame me if yer dog wants a chat,' he counters, as if he's chaffing in a public bar.

'Are you scared? Is that why you can't stop?' I see his mouth twitch and know I'm right. 'I'll leave you here if you don't hold your tongue,' I whisper. Then I turn my back on him and forge ahead, wishing that he was Pedlar, who had sharp teeth and no fear and never spoke out of turn. I'd have been safer with Pedlar, gun or no gun.

My poor boy. My brave dog.

Suddenly, to the nor'east, there's a faint cry followed by a sharp crack.

That's not a musket. That's a pistol.

Gyp's head jerks up.

'Christ!' Rowdy cringes. 'He's seen us!'

I shake my head. Whoever fired that gun, he's well out of range. Perhaps a snake frightened him.

I was right about the signals, though; that last one sent him downstream. Now we just have to reach the road before he turns back.

The question is: should we stay by the river? It winds about like a snake's trail and that's good, because nobody a quarter-mile downstream can look back along the riverbed and see us. But it will make our journey longer—and we don't have much time. What if someone catches up with Queenie? What if she loses the red shirt?

I think we should cut through the bush here.

'This way,' I tell Rowdy, and plunge into a thicket.

I'd be more anxious doing this if Carver had a poacher's eye. Not that we're leaving footprints, in our sheepskin boot-soles, but on a stony riverbank there are no branches to break or thorns to snatch at stray hairs. You don't have to worry about tell-tale threads getting caught on twigs. You don't have to trample the undergrowth.

Those are the signs I always look for when I'm stalking: threads, hairs, crushed moss, broken bushes. But Carver isn't trained to hunt like me. He was born in Portsmouth, with his eyes turned to the sea, and was lagged for robbing a coach. So Carver looks for a different set of signs: weakness, wealth, seclusion. I'm hoping Cockeye's the same. I'm hoping they won't know a fresh scuff-mark when they see one.

Besides, the important thing here isn't stealth. The important thing is speed.

Suddenly the air fills with parrots, flushed from a covert. They shoot up like fireworks, screeching and flapping and making Gyp bark. She can't help it; she's been taken by surprise.

This is bad.

Two shots ring out.

'Christ!' Rowdy hisses from behind me. 'Did Carver see that?'

Of course he saw it—and heard it, too. That's why he's signalled to Cockeye. We might as well have lit a bonfire.

'Run!' I crash forward. Gyp takes the hint, racing along ahead of me, quicker now that she's free of her sheepskin. She vanishes into the thick growth up ahead.

Rowdy yelps in pain as if he's stubbed his toe.

And here's the river again, winding back across our path. Gyp's already on the opposite bank, waiting for me. The ground's uneven, all rocks and puddles, and it slows me down. Rowdy trips and drops his carbine.

God help us. 'If you can't look after that, give it to me,' I tell him, though I don't really want the gun. Not now. Carver's first target will be the man with the gun.

'I'll mind it better, I swear,' Rowdy says, scooping it up.

Gyp joins me as I plunge back into the bush, which isn't so dense on this side of the river. I've a map in my head and if I'm reading the sun like a seaman, the ford is in front of us, to our right. The hill, of course, is on our left. And the road stretches between 'em, with Carver's horse on it somewhere.

Pray God we find that horse.

Gyp yaps ahead of me. I can't even see her; there's a tea-tree blocking my view. But when I burst through to the other side, I find myself in a clearing with a small knot of sheep. They're huddled together, bleating: Floss, Birdie, Echo and Sage.

Sage doesn't look well. The wool on her back is singed.

'We should hide,' Rowdy gasps, stumbling out of the bush to my rear. 'Is there somewhere we can hide and wait for Barrett's men to come?'

Hide and eat what? Shoot a sheep and Carver will find us. Light a fire and Carver will find us. He won't leave this place—not until we're dead.

No witnesses.

Gyp seems keen to gather the sheep, but comes to heel when I click my tongue. Together we cross the clearing, which must have been made by the death of a great tree—we have to scramble over the rotten remains of the trunk before we reach cover on the other side. There's brush here, too, though not as much of it. And that, if I'm not mistook, is a cross-cut stump.

We must be close to the road.

'Look!' says Rowdy, pointing at the stump.

Yes, I saw it.

We pass another stump—and another. The trees are thinning out. Beyond them I can make out a clear patch, like a garden glimpsed through a picket fence.

Motioning to Rowdy for silence, I hunker down and start to crawl. Gyp slips along beside me, brushing my arm with her tail. At last we reach the road, which is pinched between swathes of forest that seem intent on swallowing it up. A pair of narrow wheel-tracks are separated by a ribbon of uncut grass. To my right, in the distance, a stone-lined dip marks the position of the ford where the road crosses the river. There's nothing else to see on that stretch: no Carver, no Cockeye, no horses. No men from Mr Barrett, either, but I wasn't expecting any.

When I turn my head there's movement to the south, across the road. Three horses stand in the shade with their reins draped over a stump, flicking their tails to keep the flies off.

Beside them, in silhouette, a figure sits with his back against a tree, his chin on his chest, his cabbage-tree hat pulled down low over his eyes.

That looks like the man I shot at.

⧺

My brother was six years older than me. There was a sister between us, but she died young. My mother never delivered her fourth child. She perished with the babe. After that, there was no one left to stand between me and my brother Jack.

He had a hard streak and called me a runt. While I was still poaching pheasant's eggs, he was already coursing hares. When I was given my first dog, he was given his first gun. As the elder son, he had his pick of the bedding, the bread and the puppies, and took it as his due. But he also bore the brunt of my father's temper.

Though we were both of us beaten, I never had my nose

broke or one of my teeth knocked out as my brother did. He was toughened by my father's anger: tempered, as wood can be hardened by fire. When we fought he always won. He used me to flush partridges sometimes, and would fire so close that splinters grazed my skin. Once he and his two friends—Fleming the butcher's son and a farmhand called Turnip—threw me into a bull's pen to see how fast I could run. Once my brother tried to set his dog on me, but the beast was my friend and did no more than half-heartedly worry my ankle.

Later, in the coverts, we were all three of us hunting deer—my father, my brother and I. I had a gun by then: an old blunderbuss with a loose stock and no great range. It was good only at close quarters, but that suited me, for I was lighter than I am now, and quiet as a fox. I could creep up on anything, furred or feathered. I could even creep up on trout.

That evening, I crept up on my brother. I could have shot him where he stood. I had the muzzle aimed at the back of his neck, but I didn't fire. I couldn't. For one thing, he was my brother. Though much of the time I loathed him, there was a blood connection so deep that when I learned he'd been shot in the head by Colonel Newton's gamekeeper, I was seized by a splitting headache that lasted for three days. I remember how badly it throbbed while I was creeping about the Elveden estate at night, springing traps, unstopping earths and doing everything I could to ruin the management of the colonel's game. Perhaps it was guilt I felt, more than grief, but whatever it was, it couldn't have been fiercer. Though I often hated Jack, I couldn't have killed him, any more than I could have killed Obadiah Johnson, or Dan Carver, or the magistrate who sentenced me. The fact is, I don't have the stomach for slaughter.

I've never killed anyone. Not even the man I shot at.

⌗

'Jaysus!' Rowdy hisses into my ear. 'That's never Nobby?'

Nobby. I'd forgotten his name.

'He was shot!' Rowdy continues. 'I saw it! He can't be alive!'

'Is that Raisin?'

'What?'

'That looks like Raisin.' I'd know her anywhere: the bay mare with the chipped ear. Beside her, Bolivar is the blue roan gelding with black points. The third horse is Woodbine, a sorrel mare with a white snip on her muzzle.

'What are ye talkin' about?' Rowdy whispers.

I have to turn my head to study his face, which is crumpled into a frown. Surely he must recognise at least one of 'em?

'Don't you know them horses?' I ask him quietly.

They're Mr Barrett's.

He opens his mouth, but before he can speak there's a rustle in the bushes to our left. We both duck, flattening ourselves against the forest floor—and watch as a sheep spills out onto the road, halfway between us and the horses.

Birdie must have followed us.

'Baa-aa,' she says.

Suddenly Echo appears behind her, bleating. And there's Floss and poor Sage.

Rowdy elbows me in the ribs. He's trying to tell me something: that Nobby hasn't moved, perhaps?

The sheep are all making a bee-line for the horses, whose ears twitch in response. But Nobby remains motionless.

'Is that cove asleep?' Rowdy asks under his breath. 'Or does he want us to think he is?'

I don't know. The horses shift nervously. Woodbine snorts. Raisin tosses her head.

'Might be an ambush,' Rowdy points out. 'He might have a gun.'

I don't see how. Last time I counted, Carver had three guns: a duelling pistol and two muskets. We took his carbine.

'Is he trying to lure us in?' Rowdy continues, because every thought that enters his head seems to leave it instantly through his mouth. But he's right. This could be a trap.

The sheep wander towards Nobby, veering away only when Bolivar stamps his hoof. Still Nobby doesn't look up. He doesn't even twitch.

I can't see him well enough.

'We need to get closer,' I tell Rowdy.

He nods. 'Send Gyp.'

Send Gyp? Over my dead body. Rowdy starts to gabble when I glare. 'That dog's a smaller target!' he hisses. 'If she's quick, she'll reach him long before he can fire, and will keep him busy while we're closin' in—'

I cut him off by crawling away. We're not using Gyp as a shield, thank you very much. Toss her in front of a pistol ball just to save our own skins? I think not.

She follows me through the scrub as I inch my way towards

Nobby, her head and haunches well down. I'm making too much noise with all my crackling and rustling, but Nobby doesn't react. Raisin does—her head swings in my direction. She scans the leafy screen in front of me.

Nobby stays as still as a steeple.

I can hear Rowdy bringing up the rear. He's even noisier than I am. But the sheep are bleating, and that helps. So does the cackle of a laughing jackass. When I reach the grove of saplings opposite Nobby, I've already made up my mind. I don't need to see the drag-marks in the dirt near him, or the cloud of flies buzzing around his hat.

Nobby's no threat to us.

'He's dead,' I tell Rowdy, who's settling into the scrub at my side.

For once he's speechless. All he does is blink.

'Steady,' I murmur to Gyp, as I grope for a rock. She pricks up her ears. To Rowdy I say, very softly, 'Is that gun primed?'

He nods.

'Shoot him if he moves,' I add, straightening. Beside me, the muzzle of the carbine swings up. There are sheep between me and Nobby, so they'll give me some cover.

I signal to Gyp with a closed fist.

'Away!' I tell her—and together we burst out onto the road.

She reaches Nobby just ahead of my rock, which lands between his outstretched legs. Still he doesn't move. Gyp confronts him with a growl, all bared teeth and raised hackles, but he doesn't lift his head.

Keeping low, I push through the knot of sheep and slowly circle the tree that's propping him up until I'm right behind him. Raisin whinnies. Flies drone. There's no weapon here; Nobby's hands lie empty, their fingers curled.

Reaching around the tree trunk, I flip off his hat.

Ugh.

'Holy Mary mother o' God,' says Rowdy, as he steps out of the scrub.

Nobby's got no face—just shattered teeth, bone chips and dried blood under a gleaming blanket of flies. Carver's left a dead man to guard his horses.

'Will ye not put his hat back on?' Rowdy begs, turning away with a grimace. I don't blame him. I don't want to look at this, either. I replace the hat.

No wonder the animals are skittish.

'Come on.' We need to go. While Rowdy cautiously advances, glancing up and down the road, I unhitch Raisin and lay a soothing hand on her muzzle. Then I flick the reins over her ears.

She's saddled and sweaty, like the other horses. Stirrups dangle. Saddlebags are well-stuffed. I'd check inside 'em if I had time to unbuckle the straps, but I don't.

I'm adjusting the stirrups when a shot splits the air.

Dust spurts up at Rowdy's feet. He's unhitching Woodbine, and causes her to jib when he flinches. Swinging myself into Raisin's saddle, I spot Cockeye. He staggers out of the bush across the road, salting his priming pan.

'Go! Go!' Rowdy yells at me. Gyp is snarling and ready to pounce—but I can't let her do it because who knows where Carver might be? I whistle her away, tugging Raisin's head around.

Rowdy hauls himself up onto Woodbine. Cockeye tamps down his powder.

I drum my heels into Raisin's flanks.

She springs forward as I look back. That's when Cockeye shoots.

The ball hits Bolivar.

'*No!*' The horse falls to his knees, screaming, and that terrible sound is like a knife in my heart. But the crack of the carbine drowns it.

Cockeye ducks. Rowdy's ball hits a tree.

Now Woodbine's galloping after me, with Rowdy low in the saddle. (Bad seat. Too much grip.) Gyp's streaking along, mouth open, tongue flapping, but she's starting to fall behind Raisin. I hope she minds Woodbine because Rowdy won't mind her.

Bolivar. Poor Bolivar. Pray God Cockeye shoots him dead before he suffers any more pain...

A gun fires, but it wasn't Cockeye's. Where did that come from?

We're pounding towards the foot of the hill. The road kisses its westernmost point, then swings around it in a loop before veering south again. There's barely any cover on this end of the hill; the steep slope is all tawny grass and grey rocks with just a scattering of wind-blunted timber.

Someone's on the hillside. A dark dot, trickling towards the road.

Carver.

I push my pelvis forward and Raisin responds, hurtling along, leaving Gyp in a cloud of dust. Gyp's a smaller target than Raisin. I need to get Raisin past that hill before we're in range of Carver's muskets.

Come on, my beauty, *come on.*

She knows she's in danger. She heard Bolivar scream. But the road's too rough for a racing gallop. It jars her gait— I have to pull her back into a canter.

Carver fires. Raisin jibs. God ha' mercy, that was close. We're rounding the hill now and I've a clear view of Carver, for all I'm being thrown about like a cork on the sea. He's running straight at us, slipping and sliding. He has a gun in each hand—two long black sticks. He slings one of 'em over his shoulder, raises the other one and fires.

I feel the jolt as if the ball has hit my own body.

8

THE WORLD'S upended. I'm flying through the air and then down. Breathless.

Stars.

The darkness evaporates like mist. There's the sky and the hilltop. And what's that noise? Is it Gyp whining?

Raisin. Where's Raisin?

When I sit up, pain shoots down my left arm. Did I break something? Gyp whimpers. Raisin…

Raisin's flailing on the ground. She's been shot and there's blood everywhere.

My voice cracks when I say her name.

Suddenly I'm blinded by dust as Woodbine skids to a halt nearby.

'Quick! Up here!' Rowdy's leaning towards me, his hand outstretched. He's lost his sheepskin.

I've lost mine too. Where is it?

'Tom, hurry!'

But what about Raisin?

Carver's next shot makes Woodbine flinch and tremble. Rowdy grabs the reins to steady her. Gyp is barking hysterically.

Carver's coming. I can see him. He's reached the base of the hill.

'*Now*,' screams Rowdy.

Getting up is a strain. My leg hurts. My arm hurts. By the time I'm on my feet Rowdy is already reloading his carbine, shaking the ball into the muzzle.

Carver must be reloading too.

'Ow. Ahh…' Sticking my right foot in the stirrup puts pressure on my injured left knee. I can't use my left leg to push myself up. I can't use my left arm to pull myself up.

'Here.' With a final jab of the ramrod, Rowdy finishes reloading. Then he slings the carbine over his naked shoulder and slides to the ground. 'Grab the pommel!' he orders, clamping his hands around my waist.

Why is he doing this? Why did he stop for me? He's putting his life at risk, and for what? For someone he barely knows…

'One…two…three…heave!' He's stronger than he looks. All at once I'm in the saddle and Gyp is still barking and Carver—Carver's across the road, aiming his gun. There's a crack and a puff of smoke.

Gyp yelps and falls silent. I turn. She's flipped over. Oh God.

'Ah, Jaysus,' says Rowdy.

I try to dismount but he's in my way. 'I'll get her!' he says and turns to scoop her up. I can't see for the tears. Where's Carver? Where is he?

I'm going to kill him.

There he is, reloading: he's just stepped out onto the road. I need the gun but my hands are shaking and my arm hurts and how the hell am I going to aim?

'Tom!' Suddenly Gyp's lying across my lap. Rowdy put her there. He's hauling himself up behind me; Woodbine staggers under the extra weight but doesn't buckle.

Gyp's still breathing—whimpering—alive. She's alive.

Rowdy kicks the horse into a gallop. Gyp's eyes roll. There's blood on my hands but I can't find her wound. Where is it? 'She's shot...she's shot...'

'She'll be all right,' says Rowdy.

Please God, don't let her die. When I kiss her head she tries to lick me.

The musket cracks again, not so loud this time.

'Christ,' Rowdy mutters. He's pressed against my back, his chin on my scalp, his arms encircling me. He's wedged so tight in the saddle that the pommel's digging into my gut. Gyp's clasped to my chest, cradled like an infant, shuddering with every jolt. Her heart beats next to mine.

'At least he can't chase us,' Rowdy croaks. 'Not without horses.'

Raisin. Bolivar.

Gyp.

I can't bear it. The sobs come tearing out.

'Ah, now. Don't fret. They'll mend her at the farm,' Rowdy offers. 'We just have to get there.'

With a nudge of his heels, he urges Woodbine forward. She's already labouring; her hoofs hit the ground like cannon balls as she canters along.

'Stop it.' Can't you feel the strain on her? 'Slow down.'

'What?'

'Slow down or you'll kill the horse!'

Our pace eases as Rowdy shifts in the saddle behind me. I think he must be looking over his shoulder.

'You're right,' he says. 'They'll not catch up now. Not on foot.'

I don't care if they do—not if Gyp dies. Woodbine's gait slows even further, to a running walk. We've rounded the hill and are leaving it behind, following the southward sweep of the road. The bush is closing in again.

'D'ye think they'll leave off?' Rowdy asks. I wish he'd stop talking; Gyp needs me. She needs everything I have.

But Rowdy was there when I needed him; he saved my life. So I answer his question by shaking my head. Leave off? Why would Carver leave off?

'They must know we're heading for Mr Barrett's,' Rowdy counters. 'Why wouldn't they cut and run?'

'No witnesses,' I answer hoarsely.

'Eh?'

'Carver was lagged on account of a witness he left alive. He told me he'd never make the same mistake again.'

'Aye, but he'd be mad to follow us,' Rowdy argues. His voice sounds shaky. His breathing quickens. 'There'll be guns at Mr Barrett's, and a deal more folk—'

'We don't know that.'

'Sure, we'll have an army to fight for us—'

'Are you blind? Or just stupid?' God ha' mercy, I shouldn't speak so harsh, but we're marked for slaughter…and Gyp's dying…and I can't bear it, I can't…'We're on Mr Barrett's horse, you fool!'

Rowdy gasps.

'Don't you know her? Didn't you work the horses at all?' People don't care. They don't look. They pass by without seeing the beasts all around 'em. 'Check in the saddlebags.'

'The saddlebags?'

'*Check inside.*'

With the saddle pitching and rolling beneath him like a ship's deck, Rowdy has a hard time reaching either of the saddlebags. All the same, he gropes for the buckles by his left knee. Gyp's panting. Her eyes are on mine—she wants me to stop the pain.

'Shh…that'll do. That'll do, my good girl…'

'Hell and damnation,' says Rowdy. He's pulled something from the starboard saddlebag. Something else hits the ground; he must have dropped it. An apple? I can't be sure. We've already left it far behind.

Rowdy thrusts a silver cruet under my nose and I bat it aside. I don't want it between me and Gyp.

'D'ye recognise that?' Rowdy demands.

I nod.

'Is it Mr Barrett's?'

I nod again.

'Mother o' God.'

I whisper in Gyp's ear. I tell her I'm with her. I tell her she's safe. I tell her I won't leave. The forest slides past, but it means nothing to me. I don't know how far we've come and I don't care.

'So they went to the farm first,' Rowdy says at last. When I don't answer, he adds, 'They might have done it at night. Slipped in without rousin' a soul. Killed the dogs. Rifled the kitchen and no one the wiser...'

Oh, I'm sure. And cleaned up after themselves. And locked the doors. And fed the chickens.

There's nothing good left—nothing. Please God, take this cup from me.

I don't know what to do.

⧾

When I first saw Gyp, I'd just arrived at the farm. I was waiting by Mr Barrett's stables as he talked to George Trumble about the supplies that needed unloading from the wagon. All the dogs had run up to greet their master. Scylla was there. Nugget. Rex. Lion.

Gyp was there, too, a little behind the others. She was the only dog who didn't bark at me. After the rest of 'em had sniffed my boots and run off to inspect Mr Barrett's purchases, Gyp stayed behind, studying my face with eyes the colour of treacle. When the overseer showed me to my bed, she followed us—until he sent her away. But she came back later, while I was mucking out the stables. And again that night, after dinner. And again in the morning.

She was half-trained. Mr Barrett knows dogs but he's a busy man. He never had much time for Gyp. The others were too ignorant and heavy-handed to train her up. They hadn't the wit or the patience.

I used my own rations and snared a few birds and soon Gyp was coaxed into the right habits. I never had to use a stick, because she was so clever. Mr Barrett noticed. He approved. He told the other lags that they should take their cue from me; my life was a misery from then on. Charlie and Jim shunned me and taunted me and did their best to damage my prospects. I wasn't the one who wet my bed or let the chickens out. Charlie did that—and lied about it after.

Mr Barrett should have realised I wasn't to blame, but he's like a man blind in one eye who doesn't see the full picture and won't turn his head to look. Why should he? To him, we're part of the fixtures. If we're faulty we can be replaced. Though he prefers us to the blacks, he doesn't care enough to dispense proper justice. For a sworn magistrate, he's far too hasty.

The magistrates at my trial were the same. It was all over in a few minutes. When someone said, 'The Queen against Clay,' I knew I'd lost, because who'd lay a bet on a contest between the Queen and a twelve-year-old Suffolk poacher? Then the underkeeper, Cocksedge—he'd been promoted to head keeper after Clegg's death— mentioned that he was the one who'd apprehended my father. Then the parish constable told the court that, in my case, the apple hadn't fallen far from the tree. He talked of my father, my brother and my Uncle John, transported for poaching five years before, who died of consumption on the way to New South Wales. Poaching was in our blood, the constable said: we were the most notorious poaching family in a notorious poaching village.

No one spoke for me. Courts don't work like that. Even Tobias from the beer shop stayed silent; he wasn't about to admit he'd been buying stolen trout and partridges. When asked if I had anything to say, I couldn't find my voice. It had deserted me, along with my wits.

The magistrates sentenced me to seven years. They were trying their next case—'The Queen against Lovett'—before I'd even left the courtroom.

God knows I'm no stranger to unfair punishment. It's the way of the world. You must endure it as best you can, but the burden is always lighter when you have a friend to share it with you.

Whenever I was punished unfairly at Mr Barrett's farm, Gyp comforted me. She slept in my bed and ate at my feet. She helped me to track snakes, gather sheep, scare crows, find chickens. She protected me. She understood me. She loved me. And now she's going to die.

⧓

The light tells me we've come a long way—the light and Woodbine's weary tread. The shadows have swallowed the road. Woodbine is so tired that her head is bobbing and she's overreaching. The change in her gait is what finally pulls my eyes away from Gyp.

Gyp's unconscious but still breathing. Thank God she's still breathing.

'We're close,' I mutter. Behind me, Rowdy jerks upright; he was swaying a little, earlier. Was he drifting into a doze? He must have been—he hasn't said a word for at least an hour.

He wouldn't have had much sleep last night.

'Whassat?' he gurgles.

'We're close.' I recognise the meadow where Mr Barrett has been clearing timber. I recognise that filled pothole—I filled it myself. I recognise the sweep of the cart tracks as they curve around an outcrop of boulders.

Gyp and I have trudged up and down this patch of road many times.

'How much longer, d'ye think?' Rowdy asks.

'Not long.' Not long before I can wash Gyp's wound, and dress it, and lay her down in front of the kitchen fire. She needs water, too. There's no water in the saddlebags. There's rum and cheese and tea-cake—Rowdy's sampled all three—but no water to wash Gyp's wound or wet her tongue.

Rowdy shivers. The temperature's dropping now and he must be getting cold with no shirt on his back. Goosebumps bloom on the scarred forearms draped around my waist like a sword belt. The reins hang limp in his grasp.

And here's the edge of the farmyard, which is full of stumps and rocks. The road swings by it, throwing off a driveway that leads straight up to Mr Barrett's front door. I've grown accustomed to the style of house in this country, and the low-hanging verandas that I found so odd at first.

Mr Barrett's house has a wide veranda on all four sides; also a shingle roof, slab walls and two brick chimneys.

Neither of the chimneys is smoking.

'Hello?' Rowdy calls. 'Mr Barrett?'

No one answers; no dogs bark. That's bad. A loose chicken scurries across the road. From where we are, I can't see the kitchen because the house is in the way. But I can see the stables, set well back to the right of the house. The stable door has been left open. At the building's gable end, a rope dangles from the lift-beam above the entrance to the hayloft. Spinning slowly at the end of this rope is Nugget the wolf-hound, hanged.

'Mother o' God,' says Rowdy.

Broken bottles litter the front steps of the house. One of the windows is cracked. As we slowly advance, passing to the west of the front parlour, a small hut with cob walls becomes visible. This is the cool-room, lying between the stables and the kitchen. Pools of dried blood stain the ground in front of it. Behind it, a cow lies motionless in the thick grass of the southern paddock, her belly bloated with gas. Poor Buttercup.

'Christ,' Rowdy whispers.

'Stop.' I need to take Gyp inside. I don't know what we'll find there, but Gyp is my only concern.

Rowdy brings Woodbine to a halt and dismounts, nervously clutching the carbine.

'*Hello?*' he yells.

Nothing stirs save Nugget's revolving corpse and another chicken—Mrs Munns—bustling through the vegetable garden, which lies between the kitchen and the rear of the house. She's picking at turnip greens.

The garden's picket fence has been flattened in one corner, as if by a falling bullock.

'Look,' says Rowdy. He points at a paper cartridge-tail trembling on the ground. It flits away in the fitful breeze as I glance down at it.

In front of us, the rickety kitchen is propped up by an enormous stone chimney that isn't smoking. I've never known Mrs Trumble to let the kitchen fire go out.

'Here,' says Rowdy, reaching up for Gyp. I pass her to him gently, then slide down to take her back.

My knee's much better now, but my injured arm won't bear her weight. After a failed attempt, I have to leave her in Rowdy's arms.

'Where d'ye want her?' Rowdy asks, his gaze jumping about like a flea. I lead him towards the kitchen, past an upended bucket and a single shoe. I know that shoe. It belongs to Mrs Trumble.

Slowly the kitchen door creaks open beneath the pressure of my hand. There's no one inside—save for a nut-brown pullet called Lady Jane squawking in a cage on the dresser. The smashed plates, overturned chair and upended dish of stew tell me that something bad happened here.

A hanging pot-rack dangles from two hooks instead of four, as if someone has been swinging on it.

'There,' I tell Rowdy, pointing at the scuffed boards in front of the hearth. 'Put her there.' The embers in the fireplace are black and cold but I can always build a new fire to warm Gyp.

'Where are they?' asks Rowdy, as he lowers Gyp onto the floor.

I don't answer. Now that Gyp is stretched out I can see where she's been shot. The ball has passed straight through her hindquarters.

Surely that's a good thing? At least she wasn't shot in the heart or the head…

'Perhaps they ran away,' Rowdy mutters.

A copper pan has fallen from the pot-rack. I pick it up and dip it into the water-bucket that stands permanently near the stone sink. Then I grab a dishcloth, soak it, place the pan near Gyp's head, gingerly dab at her wound with the cloth…

When she twitches I pull back. *Sorry. I'm so sorry.*

'You stay here. I'll go and look,' Rowdy offers. 'You should bar the door when I leave—don't let anyone else in.' He turns to go, his gaze lingering for a moment on the knife by the dresser.

'Woodbine,' I tell him, so he won't forget. Woodbine can't be left sweaty and saddled. She needs water. She needs oats and a good rub-down.

'Aye. I'll tend to her.' Rowdy hesitates. 'Bar the door,' he says again. 'Tom? You've no gun. Bar the door.'

Yes, I heard. Bar the door. Gyp's breathing has changed. Her eyelids flutter. I squeeze a trickle of water into her mouth and tuck my jacket under her head. *Please God, save her. Please God, don't let her die.*

Lady Jane is rattling her cage. She must need tending as well, after two days without food or water or room to move. It could have been worse, though: I'll wager someone was going to wring her neck and roast her.

I have to let her out. But first I have to find a blanket.

There are blankets in the hut behind the kitchen—through the back door, past the hen-house, between ranks of young fruit trees. The hut hasn't changed. No one has mended the hole in the roof or the creaky board on the threshold. No one has whitewashed the grey slab walls. My old bed's still in one corner. My old mattress. My old blanket. Whoever's been using them recently must stink like a goat.

A full chamber-pot sits under Charlie's bed, but there's no sign of Charlie or Jim or the new hand. Charlie's keepsakes are strewn about like seedpods under a tree. He never could keep a tidy berth. His woomerang was captured on Mr Barrett's first raid, which Charlie called 'beating the coverts'. As far as I can tell, Mr Barrett's party must have beat more than coverts, for they brought back many things: shells, nets, spears, spear-throwers. Charlie often complained that Mr Barrett hadn't let 'em bring back women.

Carver was part of that raid: he brought back a human ear.

I was at the farm, waiting, when Mr Barrett returned from his second raid. His notion was that if he confiscated the blacks' weapons, they were less likely to threaten us. I could have told him that they wouldn't be able to feed themselves either, but it hardly needed saying. Perhaps that was also his intention. At any rate, Mr Barrett burned a lot of spears in the farmyard that day. But Charlie kept the wooden dish he'd brought back with him.

Looking around, I can see that there must have been another raid since I left, because a stone axe is hanging on the wall. Has Mr Barrett been having trouble with the blacks? They certainly haven't been bothering us. Sometimes I wonder if Mr Barrett organises a raid whenever he feels out of sorts. My father used to beat me when he was angry with the world; there was nothing fair or reasoned about his punishments.

Of course, Mr Barrett had his reasons for the raids: stolen sheep the first time, a neighbour's murdered shepherd the next. But I wonder if he's developed a taste for such pursuits.

Back out of the hut again, with the blanket tucked under my good arm, I spot Rowdy leading Woodbine towards the stables. I won't go looking for bandages—I don't want to leave Gyp a second time. Why not cut up another dish-cloth? That's what I'll do. They can't flog me for cutting up a dishcloth.

'Here, Gyp. Here, girl. This'll keep you warm.' There's kindling in the basket by the kitchen hearth, so I can easily lay a fire. I don't care if Carver sees the smoke. It's Gyp I care about.

Would a dose of rum dull her pain?

She wheezes as I tuck the blanket around her. Her eyes open a crack. What about laudanum? Mr Barrett has laudanum. He keeps it in his bedroom; I saw him go and fetch it once when George Trumble broke his arm.

Should *I* go and fetch it?

'Does it hurt too much?' I ask Gyp. Perhaps I should give her the laudanum. She may need it when I bandage her wound. But I don't know what the dose should be—not for a dog. You can kill someone with laudanum.

I stroke her head lightly. She tries to lick my hand; stiffens; gasps.

'Gyp?'

Her eyes widen. Her limbs tremble and her back arches.

'Gyp!'

Her body goes limp.

No. Oh, God.

She's left me.

⊬

I didn't watch my mother die. I wasn't allowed to. My father wanted to spare me the sight of her blood—or so he claimed. Perhaps I slipped his mind.

I saw her later, when her face was clean, her hair was combed and her hands were crossed on her breast. She'd never looked so pale. Someone had tied a strip of cloth under her chin to keep her mouth shut. Someone had closed her eyes. She wasn't dressed in her finest because her finest had been sold. It was a bad time, then. The brass bed she prized was the only piece of furniture in the room.

We were living above the Mackerel's Eye in Ixworth High Street. The midwife got drunk downstairs afterwards. So did my father.

I didn't kiss my mother goodbye, because she wasn't

there. I could see that well enough. Why say goodbye when she couldn't smile back?

I wish I could have said goodbye. I wish I'd been allowed in the room.

If she had anything to tell me before she breathed her last, I never heard it.

9

AFTER MY mother died I was all alone. It's the same now.

Why would God take Gyp and leave Carver?

Her fur is wet where I've been crying into it.

I've no dog.

What am I going to do?

+⊢

'Tom!'

Rowdy's knocking.

'Tom!' He knocks again. There's a creak of hinges. 'Chrissake, I told ye to *bar* this door!' His footsteps sound uneven, as if he's limping. His voice cracks. 'I—I found the others,' he says brokenly. 'They're in the meat-house. They...'

He trails off. More footsteps. He's standing near me; the air shifts.

I don't look up.

'Ah, no,' he murmurs. His knees crack as he squats down. His gun hits the floor. 'I'm sorry, lad. I'm so sorry. She was a good dog.'

She was more than good. She was the best. The best dog there ever was.

She's still warm. With my face buried in her coat and my eyes shut I can pretend she's still with me.

Oh, God. Oh, God.

'Listen, Tom, I know how ye feel,' Rowdy continues, 'but we can't sit here like this. Even with the horse it'll take us all o' three days to reach town and...Tom?'

Go away. I don't care. Leave me alone.

He lays a gentle hand on my shoulder. ''Tis a sore loss, indeed, but Tom—God help us—there are six slaughtered folk out in the meat-house. *Six*. Dumped in a pile like...' His voice wobbles, and he stops. I can hear him gulping down air like a drowning man. 'Jaysus,' he whispers. 'God help us all.'

He rises and goes to the sink. Water splashes. He retches and coughs, sniffs, sighs.

'If we don't lay a plan, we're lost,' he says hoarsely, coming back to crouch beside me again. 'Carver will find us. He'll find us and he'll kill us.'

'I don't care.'

'What?' He can't hear me. Not through Gyp's fur. 'What did ye say?'

'I don't care!' Sitting bolt upright, I shout at him. 'I don't care! I don't care what happens to me!'

'Well, I care!' He grabs both of my arms and gives me a shake. 'I care what happens to ye.'

'You don't.' My voice breaks on a sob. 'Why should you?'

'Because we're friends. Eh? Friends and allies.' He can talk very quickly when he wants to; the words flow out, soft and tuneful like a song. He has a fine voice. I daresay he needed a fine voice to pass fake coins in public bars. 'I'm all ye have now, and you're all I have,' he says. 'But we'll survive this together. D'ye hear?'

Survive. How am I going to survive? Gyp is dead.

'Now, I know you're not fond o' folk,' he continues. 'That's clear enough, and I don't doubt you've got yer reasons. You'd trust a beast above a man—well, I'd not fault ye on that, or on grievin' the friend who loved ye.'

She loved me. She did. I wipe away the tears as they trickle down my cheeks.

'But what would Gyp say if we were to perish?' Rowdy pushes my chin up with iron fingers and looks me straight in the eye. 'She'd not be happy. She would have given her own life to save yours, would she not?'

She did. She gave her life.

'So why would ye throw it away?' Rowdy demands. 'Why would ye throw away somethin' that Gyp valued above her own life, as if it means nothin'? D'ye think she'd thank ye for it?'

No. She wouldn't.

'Seems to me ye should honour her by staying alive,'

Rowdy murmurs. He releases my chin and puts his hand on my head. I used to do the same with Gyp, to calm her. 'Seems to me there's other beasts need yer help. What about the horse? I've done me best with her, but...'

Woodbine. Has he dried her off? Has he put a blanket on her?

'We have to act, Tom,' Rowdy insists. 'And we have to do it before Carver gets here.'

When I nod, his hand drops from my head. I have to swallow and clear my throat before I can speak.

'I'm going to kill Dan Carver.'

'Aye, but we'll need guns to do that,' Rowdy observes. 'Where does Mr Barrett keep his guns?'

What? 'Don't you know?'

Everyone used to know where Mr Barrett kept his guns. He hung 'em over the mantels in his parlour and dining room. Each time a black passed by, or a dog scared a snake, or a mounted man rode up to the front door, Mr Barrett would dash inside and fetch one of his muskets. Every time he wanted to hunt ducks, or kill a maimed sheep, or raid a blacks' campsite, he would sit on the front veranda, cleaning and polishing one gun or the other.

Didn't Rowdy ever see him do it?

'Sure, and I wasn't here more 'n two days before Mr Barrett sent me off to the hut,' he explains quickly, with a crooked smile. 'How long were ye here yerself?'

'Six months.'

'Well, there ye are, then.' Rowdy snatches up the carbine and surges to his feet. 'So where are the guns?'

I don't understand. 'With Carver,' I say, peering up at Rowdy. Can he really be that stupid?

Carver stole Mr Barrett's horses. Why would he have left Mr Barrett's guns behind?

Rowdy's shoulders sag a little. His face falls as the truth hits him.

He holds up the carbine. 'Is this Barrett's?' he asks.

I shrug. No one ever gave me a gun while I was working on the farm. If there was ever a gun on offer, George Trumble always got to it first. Though Mr Barrett was as jealous of his weapons as he was proud, he would occasionally take Trumble out with him to shoot wild dogs or game. Or blacks, of course.

I don't think Charlie or Jim ever got their hands on a firearm. Mr Barrett didn't trust 'em enough.

'I don't know Mr Barrett's guns,' I have to admit. The only one I'd recognise at a glance is the shepherds' musket, because Mr Barrett gave me leave to use that.

Carver has it now.

'In that case we should search the whole farm,' says Rowdy. 'There's no tellin' what we might find in the way o' weapons.' And he extends a hand to help me up.

Oh, no. I'm not leaving Gyp. 'I have to bury my dog first.'

'But—'

'I'm going to bury my dog.' With a headstone. And flowers. And a prayer.

'Of course ye are.' Rowdy's voice softens again. 'She deserves a Christian burial—just as soon as we arm ourselves.

She wouldn't want ye undefended, Tom. What if Carver arrives in the middle o' the funeral?'

Rowdy's right. If Carver comes, he'll desecrate the grave. I have to protect it.

'Mr Barrett kept a gun in his parlour. And another in his dining room,' I explain, climbing to my feet. 'But if Carver took 'em there are other things we can use.'

Better things. Crueller things.

I'm going to kill Dan Carver.

⧾

My father carved the board on my mother's grave because he couldn't afford a headstone. He was so drunk he botched the job; folk were buying him liquor for nearly two solid days before she was buried. During that time Jack and I slept on the landing outside the room where she lay— because the room was our home, then. We didn't move to my grandmother's cottage till the shame of our bereft condition forced her hand.

She was a mean and grudging soul who hated my father almost as much as she hated his two sons, so I didn't see him for the next few months. But then, without warning, she followed her daughter into the grave. The damp in that house did for her in the end—and since the landlord was one of my father's customers, we were allowed to stay. No one but my father would have tolerated such a rundown old hovel.

We lived in the kitchen because the other rooms were full of holes. It amazes me that we didn't die of consumption, like Uncle John. There was no privy to speak of so we dumped our soil into the neighbour's privy secretly, at night.

My mother was buried in the village churchyard next to my sister. The last time I paid 'em a visit, the board was already splitting. By that time Jack was dead and my father in gaol, and I was no longer living in my grandmother's house because the landlord, a local miller, had decided to knock it down and use the stone to repair his mill. Instead I was back at the beer shop, where I was sleeping in a corner of the stables. But I took some comfort from knowing that my mother had once slept nearby. And sometimes I would spend warm nights by her grave, to keep her company.

I was very young then.

My father wasn't buried. After the hanging, he was sold to a doctor and cut up like a side of beef. I'm glad he's not lying beside my mother. She never had a moment's peace from him when she was alive. Perhaps she's at peace now.

When I kill Dan Carver I'm not going to give him a Christian burial. I'll cut him up the way the doctors cut up my father.

Then I'll feed him to the wild dogs.

⸸

There are four rooms in Mr Barrett's house. His bedroom is at the rear, to your left as you enter the back door. I've never been inside this room before; it surprises me. The bed is smaller and lower than I expected. The floorboards are bare. The pictures hanging on the walls have been cut out of books. They're mostly pictures of great houses in England—houses that look like Elveden Hall, near Ixworth. My father used to say that such houses meant nothing but trouble for the likes of us.

The only really handsome thing in the room is a big cedar campaign chest with brass handles.

'Ah,' says Rowdy, who's peering over my shoulder. He brushes past me, heading straight for the chest.

'What are you doing?' I ask. 'The guns won't be in there.'

'I know that.' Rowdy tosses me the carbine with one hand as he yanks open a drawer with the other. 'Keep lookin'. I'll be along presently.'

He pokes around and drags out a white muslin shirt.

'You're not taking that?' I say, as he pulls it over his head.

'I'm cold,' he replies, his voice muffled by its folds.

'But that's larceny!' I was lagged for less. 'They'll send you to Port Arthur.'

'I don't think Mr Barrett will miss this shirt,' he says. His head is through the collar, now, and all at once he looks sick—pale—as if he's about to vomit. He swallows hard, then adds, 'The only other shirts I've seen here...no Christian soul would ask me to wear 'em.'

I know what he's talking about. I heard the flies buzzing around the cool-room as we were walking from the kitchen to the house. They sounded like a swarm of angry bees.

Rowdy wouldn't discuss what was in that cool-room. 'Six people,' was all he'd say. 'I counted heads.'

I wonder where the rest of the dogs are. Pray God some of 'em survived—unlike Gyp. Gyp's gone. I'll never see her again.

The pain of it hits me in the gut and I'm suddenly bent double.

'Come on.' Rowdy picks up the carbine on his way out of Mr Barrett's bedroom. Across the hall, the second bedroom is even plainer than the first. It contains only an iron bedstead and a brass-bound sea-chest. When Rowdy checks inside, the chest is full of blankets.

'Nothin'.' He lets the lid crash down.

Back in the hallway, Nellie the speckled hen squawks and flutters as we drive her ahead of us. The first door we reach opens into the dining room. I've never been in this room, either. It reminds me a little of the courtroom at Bury, on account of all the polished wood. There's a big table, just like the one where the lawyers sat, and a sideboard carved like the magistrates' box, and a clock, and a hanging lamp. There's even an oil painting on the wall, though this one doesn't show a robed man in a wig. This one is a portrait of a lady who's probably Mrs Barrett.

Looking at it now, I wonder why her husband left her in England. Then I think: who would want to bring such a beautiful, delicate lady out here?

'Dammit.' Rowdy points at the empty brackets above the sideboard, which are perfectly spaced for a Brown Bess musket. Beneath them, the drawers of the sideboard have been pulled out and its doors hang open.

'Wait,' I say, as Rowdy turns on his heel. A gleaming wooden box on top of the sideboard might be a cutlery canteen—or it might be something else. 'Did Carver not have a duelling pistol with him?'

'He did.' Rowdy's whole face brightens. 'And they generally come in pairs.'

He beats me to the box by a nose, but when he flings open the lid we're confronted by a few battered pieces of monogrammed silver.

'Where would a wise man put a pistol so that Carver couldn't find it?' Rowdy muses aloud. He stoops to peer at a stack of white table linen, as if hoping to find an arsenal hidden behind it.

I'm already on my way across the hall to the parlour. I used to report to this room on occasion: Mr Barrett would sometimes call me in when he was drunk. He once had me salute the Queen there. Another time, he told me that I was a good lad, not loose-lipped like some, and that the business of the farm was *our* business, because we were all of us Englishmen, with a God-given right to defend our hearth and home. He insisted that the Queen, God protect her, would have no quarrel with those of her subjects who sought to tame a wilderness. In such a savage place, he said, even a gentleman must sometimes be savage.

I wonder now if his conscience was pricking him. Perhaps he was troubled by the floggings he'd dealt out or the blacks he'd killed. Perhaps he found me good company because I was too wary of sparking his temper to say a word. He knew that I never spoke if I could possibly help it—especially not to the other lags.

It briefly crossed my mind that he was a bugger, working up to the lunge, but I soon dismissed this notion. Though he might have been lonely, it wasn't for a boy's behind. The fact is, I could have been a stuffed bear for all the regard he paid me as he rambled on. I would stand there studying the furniture for an hour at a time. I learned the pattern of the wallpaper by heart. I came to know every creaky floorboard, every stick of furniture, every crack in the ceiling.

But now, on reaching the threshold, I freeze.

This room isn't as I remember it. The door-jamb is splintered. The window is cracked. Sprays of blood decorate the wall, the writing desk, the cushions on the settee. There are pools of blood on the carpet; flies buzz around. A clock ticks on the mantelpiece under the Queen's picture—which has been shot at, to judge from all the smashed glass.

The brackets that hang between the clock and the picture are empty. Carver's taken this gun, too.

'Holy Christ,' Rowdy croaks behind me. His hand comes down on my shoulder. 'Ye shouldn't be lookin' at this,' he says. 'Go and feel under Barrett's pillow. The pistol might be in his bed.'

He steers me back into the hallway. Why does he think me so squeamish? Where does he think I've been for the last eighteen months, Kensington Palace?

But it might be true that Mr Barrett kept a pistol close while he slept, so I retrace my steps to his bedroom, where I toss his pillows and thrust a hand beneath his feather mattress. I even search the drawers of his campaign chest, which are full of wonderful things: silk cravats, satin waistcoats, a pair of spectacles, a silver-backed looking glass, a snuff box, a bottle of laudanum...

But no duelling pistol.

'Tom!' Rowdy calls to me from the parlour. He sounds

excited. In the hallway I pass Nellie pecking at a piece of broken glass.

'What?' I ask, from the threshold of the front room.

Rowdy has opened up Mr Barrett's little card table. I never realised there was a box concealed beneath its inlaid top, which Rowdy has somehow pushed aside, like a hinged lid, to reveal a host of small compartments containing cards, dice, loose coins, whist-markers, a pencil-stub…and a pistol.

'I thought to meself, "Well now, I've heard that gentlemen sometimes duel over a game o' cards",' Rowdy explains with a grin. 'See here—there's a hidden lever.'

Once again he gives me the carbine. Then he takes possession of the pistol, which is a beautiful thing, though very old-fashioned.

I can't see any balls or powder.

'It should take a musket ball,' Rowdy murmurs. 'They generally do.' With a wry smile and a tilt of his head, he asks, 'Would ye spare me a cartridge, like a good lad?'

There are only four left. When Rowdy sees 'em cradled in my palm, he knits his brow. 'Two each?' he suggests meekly, and I nod. Two each plus the one in the carbine. Five shots in all.

'These won't take us far,' Rowdy says as he loads his pistol. 'Five shots! I'll wager Carver's got fifty-five.'

Yes, but we have other things. Better things.

I turn on my heel.

'Where are you going?' asks Rowdy.

'To even the odds.' When I head for the door, he follows me like a faithful mastiff—down the steps, across the yard, towards the stables. The light is fading fast. 'Go and make a fire in the kitchen,' I tell him.

'But—'

'Do it.'

'Tom, we'll not be stayin'.' Rowdy stops in his tracks. 'How can we? Carver could be headin' this way—'

'The fire's for him.' I doubt that Rowdy understands, but he has faith enough to submit. While I trudge past the cool-room he retreats to the kitchen. The flies are growing sluggish as night falls, but I can hear 'em through the cool-room's closed door, humming. Somehow they've got inside.

I don't want to think about what's in there. I have to keep a clear head.

The stable door is open. Rowdy has dumped Woodbine's saddlebags on the floor and left her saddle draped over the edge of the nearest stall, which is empty. For some reason, he's put Woodbine in the very farthest box; it stands hard against the southern wall, well away from the entrance. He's rubbed her down but hasn't covered her with a blanket. He's given her hay but not oats, unless she's eaten them already. Those saddlebags need repacking.

First things first, though. I need a lantern.

Mr Barrett always kept a very tidy stable. The lanterns have their own hooks, well away from the hayloft. Sacks and barrels are piled near the hayloft, and tools hang on the opposite wall, near Woodbine's haunches: an awl, a mallet, an axe, a pitchfork. Four sets of double-irons also hang there, and one of 'em is mine. I remember the relief of it when Mr Barrett struck 'em off—top-irons first, then leg-irons—threatening to put 'em back on again should I ever disobey him.

Beside the irons, hung high, are the leghold traps. Two of 'em are bear traps, bought in case the blacks gave Mr Barrett any trouble. I don't think he's ever set 'em, though they must have cost a pretty penny. Perhaps the raids have done what he hoped the traps would do.

I have to climb onto a milking stool to reach the lower trap, which is so heavy that it nearly topples me. I cry out but keep my footing—and give Woodbine a soothing pat when she tosses her head, startled by my voice. She needs a blanket.

I'll leave the lantern here and send Rowdy back for the saddlebags.

Not wanting to lay any kind of trail, I have to carry the bear trap to the kitchen instead of dragging it. My arm still hurts, so I tote the trap on my back, stooping like a river porter. Smoke trickles from the kitchen chimney, barely visible against a darkening sky. Birds are calling. Flies are settling.

Inside, a burning lamp glows on the kitchen table. Rowdy is hunched over the hearth, feeding sticks into a fresh fire.

He turns at the sound of my footsteps. 'What in God's name is that?'

'A bear trap.' The whole room shakes when it hits the floor. 'You should fetch the saddlebags,' I tell him, reaching for the poker. 'And give Woodbine some oats. They're in the cask with the pewter pot on its lid.'

'Tom—what are ye doin'?' Before I can answer, Rowdy starts babbling nervously, 'Why do we need a fire? Why show Carver we're here? We can't stay. He'll gut us if we do. We have to leave.'

'Not yet.'

'Tom—'

'Go and fetch the bags. Now.'

He does as he's told. Somehow I'm training him, the way I trained Gyp.

Gyp.

She's lying over there, wrapped in a blanket. *I'm sorry, girl. I'm so sorry.*

'Carver will pay,' I promise her as I pry up a floorboard with the edge of the poker. A hard yank and the nails yield.

Now for the next board.

'Remember that trap I laid for the wild dogs?' I remind Gyp, using the poker like a pump-handle. Once. Twice. And there's another board raised. 'Well, Carver is a wild dog and I'm going to lay a trap for *him.*'

One more should do it. The joists creak—the wood strains—the nails flex.

There.

The trap is so big it needs a special clamp to force open its jaws. Luckily that's roped to the peg, so all I have to do is unknot the rope and apply the clamp.

Do I have the muscle? Perhaps I should ask Rowdy.

'Remember how I hung a strip of my shirt above the dog-trap?' I ask Gyp. She was there, of course; she saw what I did. 'Well—I'm going to do the same here.'

I climb onto the table, unhook the pot-rack and discard the last two pots still dangling from it. Then I fetch a ball of cooking twine and begin to hang other things from the rack: a couple of knives, a couple of spoons, a meat skewer, a tea-cup, a pan-lid, a salt cellar. I'd hang Lady Jane in her cage if she wasn't so heavy.

Lady Jane. I must let her out.

There's rope in one corner, but to thread it over the rafter I have to move the table and put a chair on top, then stand on the chair and push the weft of the rope over the warp of the rafter. Luckily, the pot-rack doesn't have to be hung very far from the door—and the roof is quite low where it meets the lintel.

Bits of bark shower down onto my head.

'Tom?' The door swings open to reveal Rowdy on the threshold, clutching a saddlebag under each arm. He stares at the pot-rack 'What are ye—?'

'Stop!' My voice is sharp. He freezes, one foot suspended over the hole in the floor.

When I point at the hole, he looks down and gasps.

'I need you to open the trap for me,' I tell him, jerking my chin. The trap is lying under the table, jaws firmly shut.

But he doesn't even look at the trap. He doesn't seem to hear me.

'What the hell is *that*?' he asks, his eyes on the jingling, jangling, glittering objects that sway and dance as I hoist the pot-rack towards the roof.

'A distraction,' I reply.

'From what?'

'From the trap.' I nod at the hole I've made. 'Once you've opened its jaws, I'll put it down there. Carver won't see it if he's looking up.'

Rowdy stares at the hole. Then he stares at the trap. Then he says, 'And just what d'ye plan to bait this trap *with*?'

I frown at him. Surely he must know the answer to that question? The fire is crackling. The lamp is burning. The pot-rack chimes gently.

'Us,' I say.

10

MY MOTHER had many friends, but they were all women, so they didn't come to her funeral. Instead they lined High Street and drew their shawls over their heads when her coffin passed.

My father was too drunk to carry the coffin. His friends did it for him. Among them was the landlord of the Mackerel's Eye and an old tosspot called Browne, who died the following spring. I can't remember who else was there; it was a long time ago. But they were very kind, for all they were seedy ne'er-do-wells who spent their nights robbing coverts and their days in the local beer shop.

My grandmother bought mourning clothes for Jack and me from a slopseller in Thetford. She sold them again straight after the funeral, but I was glad to wear a respectable suit when I buried Ma. We couldn't afford much else; there were no mutes, carriages, flowers or plumed horses. Since it was winter, I couldn't find a single wild blossom to lay on her grave.

Nine men came to church, not including the vicar. He despised my father *and* his friends, and my father despised him back. My father called clergymen 'the King's lackeys'. He said they preached charity from one side of their mouths while they sermonised against poaching from the other. He said they didn't care if you starved as long as you didn't steal.

The service was very brief, though the vicar had time to commiserate with my mother on the hard life she'd led, glaring at my father all the while. It was the last time I ever set foot in that church. My mother had gone there on occasion with Jack and me, but I took against it after she died. It was never a place I felt welcome. I would step over the threshold and worry that I smelled bad.

At the graveside my father swayed like a poplar in a high wind. He saw me crying and told me I had to be a man now.

I was all of eight years old.

╫

I've wrapped Gyp in two blankets and tied 'em with twine. I've picked lavender and wattle flowers. But I didn't make a headboard.

If I mark the grave, Carver might find it. And if he finds it, he'll ravage it.

That's why I've dug it out here, on the very edge of the southern paddock. Gyp liked this place. She liked following trails through the forest ferns and gathering sheep in the long grass. She won't be lonely, either; you can see the kitchen from where I'm standing. At least, you can see it during the day.

Now all I can see is one shining window and the faint, pinkish glow above it, where the smoke is leaving the chimney. And I can see Rowdy's lantern. He's heading this way.

My own lantern is shedding a pool of light on the raw, chopped earth at my feet.

'I'll come back,' I promise Gyp. 'I'll come back with a headboard. And more flowers.' The wattle and lavender are buried with her because I can't risk Carver seeing 'em. I'll have to stamp the grave down hard and strew it with leaves. But not until I've filled it.

When the first spadeful of dirt thudded onto Gyp's flanks, I thought the sound would break my heart. Even now, with the pit almost filled, I'm still wiping away tears.

Poor Gyp. My poor girl. All alone down there in the dark.

'Right!' Rowdy stops just a few feet away and lifts his lantern. With his face washed, his hair combed and his white shirt gleaming under George Trumble's Sunday coat, he looks like a different man. A fine, fair, respectable man.

I can see why he was able to pass false coin in pubs.

'Packed and saddled. Traps laid. Tree climbed. Dog laid to rest,' he announces. 'We need to go. The moon's full enough to see by.'

'You're a good talker.' Leaning on my spade, weary and woebegone, I find myself pleading with him. 'Will you say a few words? For Gyp?'

He frowns at me, puzzled. 'Eh?' he says.

'Something religious. As a vicar would.'

Rowdy seems taken aback. 'Chrissake, lad, I'm Catholic!' he exclaims, and retreats a step. 'That dog was a Protestant— ye only had to look at her.'

'Please.'

He hesitates. I stare at him. At last he sighs and throws a quick glance over his shoulder.

'All right,' he growls, 'but we'd best be quick.'

He sets down his pistol and his lantern. Crosses himself. Folds his hands together. 'Ashes to ashes, dust to dust,' he says, his voice low and serious, 'through the valley o' the shadow o' death this faithful dog's spirit now runs free, huntin' with the angels, may she always find a warm place by the Lord's fire and keep faithful watch o'er His lambs, amen.'

'Amen.' That was beautiful. My voice cracks as I stammer, 'Do—do you truly believe she's with the angels, now?'

Rowdy gazes down at me. His face softens. 'Dog like that? Where else could she be?'

'*You* liked her, didn't you?'

He blinks. ''Course I did.'

'You picked her up.' I daresay you stopped for me because you lacked a sharp pair of tracker's eyes. But you needn't have stopped for Gyp. You could have left her on the road, but you picked her up. 'Thank you.'

I hold out my hand. Rowdy shakes it, smiling his crooked smile. 'I only wish I could have saved her,' he says, retrieving his lantern and pistol. He turns to go.

I pick up my spade and start scraping the last of the loose dirt onto the grave mound.

Rowdy stops short. 'You've done all ye can, Tom,' he urges. 'We have to leave.'

Not yet. Not until this grave is hidden.

'Tom!' He grabs me, but I shake him off and continue to push the dirt around, my bad arm aching.

'If Carver finds Gyp, he'll do something horrible,' I say.

'If Carver finds us, he'll do somethin' worse!'

Worse than hanging us from the hayloft lift-beam? Worse than sticking a pole up our backside and roasting us?

I'm patting the mound of dirt with my spade to flatten it when Rowdy loses his temper.

'Christ, but you're a stubborn little bastard!' he snaps. 'Well, I'm not about to be gutted for the sake of a dead dog!' He waves his gun at the stables. 'That horse in there is saddled and ready. Soon as I reach her, I'll count to a hundred. If you're not headin' back by then, I'll leave without ye.'

He pauses for a moment, as if expecting me to answer. I don't. Instead I lay down my spade and pick up a handful of dead leaves.

With an impatient noise, he turns on his heel and stomps off.

If he does ride away, he'll take the road to town on Mr Barrett's horse, in George Trumble's coat. Even if Carver doesn't catch him, the townfolk'll likely string him up as a thief and a cutthroat. He was new to the farm, so they won't know him. Won't trust him.

They know me. I was twice in town with Mr Barrett. If I tell my tale they might believe it, though most free folk are disinclined to trust a lag. And what if they decide it was me killed Charlie and Jim and the Trumbles? What if they think Rowdy killed Mr Barrett for his shirt and his horse and the contents of his saddlebags?

Scattering bark and leaves over the grave, I can see little hope for either of us. Even if we survive Carver, who's to say we'll survive the troopers, or a hanging judge? I've heard about the magistrates in this colony. They're worse than the ones in England. They treat lags like mad dogs.

Of course, Rowdy might be able to talk us out of gaol, with his quick tongue. Either that or he'll talk us into an ambush. Perhaps I'd fare better without him; off the road, away from Mr Barrett's shirt and horse. Perhaps I should leave him to his own devices.

It would pain me, though, I confess.

'If I had you with me, I wouldn't need Rowdy,' I whisper to Gyp, but she can't hear me. I'm all alone save for the beasts that rustle overhead in the branches. Opossums, I'll wager.

This grave still looks sadly bare; I should dig out some clumps of grass and plant 'em on top. By the time they wither, Carver won't be around to see it.

I pick up the spade and head towards the tree-line, where a few small holes won't be noticed. I have to tread carefully, though. Very, very carefully.

I'm just about to loosen the first clod when I hear a scream of pain.

The first day I met him, Rowdy Cavanagh told me he'd been apprenticed as a lad to a fanstick maker, but that his master's cruelty had driven him away. He also told me that during the three years he'd spent uttering counterfeit coin, he had passed some eighty pounds' worth of false guineas and received back a good sixty pounds in change. He said the trick of it was to hold the landlord's eyes, so that any coins exchanged would go straight into the cash drawer unregarded. He said he had always kept his mouth moving, his teeth flashing and his hands busy while he joked, laughed and teased his way to success. Sometimes he'd pretend to be ill, or angry, or shocked from having come from an accident. Sometimes he'd rattle the barmaids by kissing 'em.

As soon as the change was in his pocket, he always moved on quickly. 'Twas important, he said, to be well out of reach before the fraud could be discovered.

He was as cunning in a tavern as I am in a covert. But one evening he'd dropped his false coin, which had rolled off the counter and landed near the barmaid's foot. On picking it up, she'd looked at it twice.

The landlord caught him before he was even out the door.

'One mistake,' Rowdy said to me, on the day of our first meeting. 'A single misstep and it ruined me life.'

One mistake. Have I made that mistake now, in not leaving this farm? Will we both be killed as a consequence?

Is that Rowdy's voice I hear, raised in torment?

The first thing I do is snuff the lantern. The next thing I do is rub dirt into my hair so it won't gleam in the moonlight. Then I fling my spade into the bush and grab the carbine, which has been sitting against a tree.

Someone is still screaming.

I head across the southern paddock, keeping low and straining my eyes in the dark. Though the moon is full and the sky clear, the shadows are dense and black—blacker without Gyp here to help me. I stub my toe. I turn my ankle. I flush a small creature that bolts away through the long grass.

Drawing closer to the kitchen, I have to shoulder the gun and drop to my hands and knees. Down here I can smell poor Buttercup, off to my left. She's beginning to rot like that dead black tucked in the tree.

The grass is just high enough to conceal me when I crawl, but if I don't raise my head above it sometimes I can't see where I'm going.

'Help! Help me!' The screeches are becoming words now. Shrill, desperate words. I don't recognise that voice. It doesn't belong to Rowdy, who's over by the stables, a dark shape flattened against its southern wall.

Thank God he had the sense to douse his lantern.

A light is showing in the kitchen's rear window—and also spilling from its front door, which I can't see from here. A long, thin, golden strip lies across the ground. I'm sure I shut that door when I left. Did Rowdy open it again? Did someone else go in?

The back door is nailed shut. I hammered the nails in myself.

'Take it o-ho-hoff!' There's that voice again, coming from the kitchen. I know who it is now. That's Cockeye's voice. 'Ple-e-ease!' he wails. 'Help me!'

Rowdy sidles up to the stable door, which is standing open. He flattens himself against the wall and cranes his neck to peer inside, his pistol cocked and raised.

'Oh God, oh God, oh God...' Cockeye gurgles. 'Carver! Come here! Come here and help me!'

Carver. He's not in the kitchen, then. What if he's in the stables? I should warn Rowdy.

But just as I start to rise from the grass, my gaze snags on Cockeye. His head appears, then his shoulders, then his chest as he slowly crawls out of the kitchen and emerges from behind its northern wall. He passes through the strip of golden light, using his elbows to drag himself along.

He has a pistol in one hand.

As he lifts his gaze, he spies Rowdy. Rowdy sees him, too. They're both holding identical pistols.

Fire, damn you, fire!

I've already cocked my carbine when Cockeye reaches out. 'Rowdy,' he whimpers. 'Please. Help!'

That's when I realise. Just look at their faces.

They know each other.

How do they know each other? From a ship? From a barracks? From a stockade? From Carver's gang?

Slowly I sink back into the long grass. Rowdy didn't recognise the horses. He didn't know where Mr Barrett kept his guns. He appeared out of nowhere yesterday, just before Carver did. He was wearing a red flannel shirt. Where did that come from? It wasn't government issue.

'My leg...' Cockeye groans. 'Rowdy, please...'

Rowdy looks terrified. He hesitates. Suddenly an invisible chicken squawks and flaps somewhere over by the house.

Christ. Is that Carver? Is he coming?

Rowdy doesn't wait to find out. He panics and darts into the stables, brandishing his gun.

'Rowdy!' Cockeye shrieks. He's in full view, now. The bear trap's jaws are clamped around his ankle, the chain and peg trailing along behind him. He's left a meandering smear of blood in his wake.

That looks bad. I didn't realise...

He'll lose his foot.

'Rowdy!' he screams, sobbing with pain.

I feel sick. Rowdy. Was he lying to me? Does he know Carver? But Carver tried to kill him. Did he defy Carver somehow? Betray him? Escape from him?

I could shoot Cockeye now, before Carver comes. I've a clean shot from here. Cockeye's lying in a spreading pool of his own blood. He's laid his head down. He's moaning, his empty hand stretched towards the stables, clawing at the dirt.

I'm shaking so much that I can't take aim—and if I miss, I'm in trouble.

Perhaps I should just creep away like a little mouse. Let Rowdy have the horse and the supplies. Let Rowdy decide what to do about Cockeye.

But I swore I'd kill Carver. I swore it.

A rustle in the long grass makes me throw myself onto the ground. Holding my breath, clutching my carbine, I wait as the rustle approaches. My gun's cocked. I'm well hidden. If that's Carver...

No. He's too heavy to move so lightly. And if he was crawling, he wouldn't be so quick.

Down here the grass is too thick for the moonlight to penetrate. Even so, I can just make out the wild dog when he passes. His eyes glint as they swivel towards me, but he doesn't break his stride. He's carrying a dead chicken in his jaws. Mrs Munns, by the look of her.

He seems to dissolve into the shadows. The grass sways and closes up behind him. He leaves a few feathers and a faint, feral smell.

So Carver wasn't over by the house after all.

A terrible scream rips through the night. I bob up to look, heart racing, and see that Cockeye's not the one who screamed. He's raised his head and is staring at the stables, eyes bulging, teeth clenched, face a knot of pain.

Another scream—fainter this time—and God help us, that's Rowdy.

He's in the stables. Carver must be in there with him. Oh God, oh God—if I shoot Cockeye, Carver'll know I'm here. It might distract him from killing Rowdy, but what if he doesn't come out? What if he waits for me to come in?

There are two cartridges in my pocket, plus one in the breach. That's one for Cockeye and two for Carver.

What am I going to do?

I can hear someone gasping and sobbing and grunting. Suddenly Woodbine emerges from the stables, all saddled up. Carver is leading her, but not from the front. He's using her as a shield, keeping level with her shoulders so that I don't have a clear shot

How does he know I'm over here?

He doesn't. He's leading Woodbine with one hand and Rowdy with the other. He's guarding his left flank with Rowdy, who's stumbling along in double-irons. I'm only catching glimpses, as Woodbine stamps and jibs, but Rowdy seems to have blood on his temple. Perhaps Carver struck him there…

Rowdy yelps when Carver tugs him forward.

'Carver…' Cockeye rasps. He lifts his head, white-faced and sweating. The muscles stand out in his neck. ''Twas in the floor,' he gasps, gesturing at the bear trap. 'I can't get it off…'

Carver takes a step forward. Rowdy cries out and God ha' mercy, there's a hay hook in his shoulder, just beneath the collar bone. Carver's tied a rope to it. Half of Rowdy's white shirt has turned as red as the flannel one he used to wear.

Carver is dressed in George Trumble's coat.

'Help me,' Cockeye pleads faintly. He's losing strength; his blood is soaking into the dirt.

Nudged along by Carver, Woodbine advances a step. So does Carver. So does Rowdy, who chokes back a sob.

I peer down the barrel of my carbine and try to take aim. But I don't want to hit Woodbine. I'm no marksman—not with a gun I've never fired.

Besides, my hands are still shaking.

'That's a bear trap,' says Carver, cool as ice. He's standing over Cockeye, gazing down at the savaged limb. 'You'd need a clamp to get that off.'

Yes, and I've hid the clamp, Dan Carver. I've hid it well.

'Oh God,' says Cockeye. He's looking worse than Rowdy, who looks bad enough. Now and then I catch sight of Rowdy as Woodbine shifts her weight; he's swaying a little and gasping for breath, his face as bleached as Cockeye's. His eyes remind me of Gyp's just after she was shot.

If he ever did run with Carver, he's regretting it now.

'Seems to me the bone's broke.' Carver is still studying Cockeye's leg. 'What do you think, Rowdy?'

Rowdy answers with a grunt.

'Nothing to say?' Carver jeers. 'You never bin lost for words before...'

He jerks at the hook and Rowdy screams.

I was right. They know each other.

'Aye, well—there's allus someone worse off.' Carver releases Woodbine, bends down and plucks the pistol from Cockeye's hand. Creeping sideways towards the kitchen, I find I can see the murderous bastard much better. He has two muskets on his back, their straps crossed on his chest. Rowdy's pistol is sticking out of his coat pocket. But this is still a bad angle. If I fire from here, I might hit Rowdy.

'Damage like that,' says Carver, shaking his head, 'is why you're better putting a beast out of its misery.'

He raises Cockeye's pistol.

'No wait!' Cockeye shrieks, just as Carver, wearing a look of feigned sorrow, shoots him in the face.

11

DAN CARVER used to claim that he'd once been a butcher.
It could have been true. Whenever we needed a fresh supply
of mutton he would always do the slaughtering, for he was a
dab hand at cutting throats and tying up entrails. He could
skin a sheep in five minutes flat.

My father also had a way with knives, like most of the
men in Ixworth. He could skin an eel or a rabbit in the dark.
Though he'd tear the skin when plucking feathers, he had
enough skill to gut a hind, if pressed. He often called himself
a butcher when asked how he earned his livelihood; a good
many poachers do.

You'd be surprised how many butchers there are in some
Suffolk villages.

But Carver outdid my father because Carver enjoyed butchering. He was always happy when he had meat to slice. He laughed about chopping off chickens' heads and nicking the arteries of pigs. He talked with relish of beating men to death.

He never mentioned shooting anyone. I would have thought it too quick an end, for a man of his tastes.

By Carver's standards, a ball in the brain can only be seen as an act of mercy.

⟊

'Tom Clay!' Carver shouts. 'I know you're out there. Rowdy Cavanagh told me so.'

He lowers his smoking pistol and shoves it into his waistband. Then he grabs Woodbine's reins, taking a step backwards.

Rowdy gasps and hisses. Cockeye lies still.

'He's a weak one, is Rowdy,' Carver continues. 'Ran away from his road gang because he couldn't take it. Ran away from me because he couldn't take it—'

'He's mad, is why!' Rowdy suddenly exclaims. 'He killed a logger—'

Carver yanks at the hook buried in Rowdy's shoulder. Rowdy squeals like a pig. Hobbled by his leg-irons, he staggers and nearly falls.

My teeth are clenched tight.

'...and he was going to run away from you because he couldn't take it,' Carver adds. I can't see him anymore. He's backing up, pulling Woodbine's head around, forcing her into a tight circle. Her haunches are shielding him now.

I creep towards the stables, keeping low, on the lookout for a clean shot.

From somewhere behind Woodbine, Rowdy screeches again. Every tug of the hook must feel like a flaming brand.

'But you're made o' flint, ain't you, Tom Clay?' Carver says loudly. 'You won't run. Not if I'm killing this here horse.'

God ha' mercy. Squinting down the barrel of my carbine, I wonder if I should shoot Woodbine and have done with it. Better a quick death than a slow one. But then Carver would know where I am. He'd come after me; he might reach me before I had time to reload...

'I was thinking I'd kill Rowdy first, but I know you'd choose the horse over him any day.' Carver's almost reached the stable door. Perhaps if I can get closer to the kitchen, the angle would improve. I'd still be scared of hitting the others, though.

'Fire away Tom,' Carver cries. 'Or don't you want to show me where you are?'

No, I don't. He has three guns, and I have one. Besides, I can't see him. He's shielded. I might have a chance from the other side of the kitchen.

'I ain't got no use for spineless folk like Rowdy,' Carver says, 'but you and I could deal together, Tom Clay. If you've the bottom for it.'

Strike a bargain with you? And have my head caved in the moment my back was turned?

I'm holding my breath as I squat in the long grass, motion-less. My eyes are screwed up into narrow slits so they don't catch the light. I'm glad I've cocked my gun. I wouldn't want Carver to hear the hammer click.

Cockeye lies not twenty yards away. His head is spread across the trodden earth in sprays and clumps of red.

I can't look at him.

'You want 'em to die, then?' says Carver, with a shrug in his voice. 'As you please. I've no objection.'

He retreats into the stables, pulling Woodbine and Rowdy along with him. The smell of fresh blood is making Woodbine skittish; she's rolling her eyes and champing at the bit. Rowdy squawks in pain.

As the stable door closes behind him, Carver adds, 'This horse won't thank you, Tom Clay. Don't think I'd baulk at killing it just to save meself a long walk.'

The door shuts.

He's going to torture Woodbine. He'll do it for his own pleasure. Then he'll kill Rowdy and take his time about it.

Breathe, Tom, breathe. Stay calm. You can't walk away; Gyp wouldn't. She was brave as a lion. She'd never have left a horse to be butchered or a friend to be murdered—if Rowdy *is* a friend. He's been lying to me. He's been keeping things from me. He was going to ride off without me, unless I'm greatly mistook.

But he doesn't deserve to die at Carver's hand.

Besides, if I walk away, I'll never be free of Carver. I'll never be able to close my eyes without worrying that he's in the shadows, waiting to attack. I need to finish this one way or another. The question is: how?

Think, Tom. What will Carver be doing at this moment?

He'll be loading his guns. He has four of 'em. One will be pointed at the stable door. Another will be pointed at the hayloft. He knows about the hayloft; he'll be expecting me to sneak in through there.

I sling my carbine over my shoulder and scurry back towards the kitchen, skirting the rear of the farmyard until I'm a couple of yards from my old hut. A quick dash across open ground brings me to the hut's eastern wall, which faces away from the stables. I'm safe here for the moment. Carver can't see me.

From the stables comes a muffled whinny, very high and shrill, then a furious thumping noise. God ha' mercy, what's that devil doing to Woodbine?

Perhaps he's not doing anything. Perhaps he's holding a gun on Rowdy and Rowdy's doing it. That's how I'd arrange matters if I were Carver. I wouldn't run any risks.

Now for the next leg. Luckily, the garden fence stretches all the way from the kitchen to the house. Bent double, I scamper along behind it until I reach the shelter of the next slab wall, then circle the house, feeling my way in the darkness and praying I don't disturb any dogs or chickens. The slightest sound would be the end of me.

My sheepskin boot-soles, though very worn, are still soft enough to keep my tread silent on the veranda boards as I creep through the front door and into the house. Outside there was moonlight; in here I have to feel my way, patting the walls, groping with my feet, wincing at every creak of the floor and every crunch of broken glass. This feels like the old days when my father would come home late from the beer shop. Drink always put him in a bad temper; I used to wait behind a collapsed pigsty until I could hear loud snoring from inside my grandmother's house. Then I would sneak through the door and slide into bed, hoping not to rouse him.

The difference here is that the house is bigger—and that my father, for all his faults, never favoured torturing folk. He certainly never stuck a hook through a man. The only living thing that he ever hooked was a fish.

At the end of the corridor I turn into Mr Barrett's bedroom. Like a blind boy I fumble about until I find the campaign chest and count the drawers from top to bottom. The looking-glass is in the bottom drawer, which squeaks slightly when I pull it out. I wince, stop, listen.

Far away in the stables, Woodbine squeals.

God damn you to hell, Dan Carver.

My questing fingers fasten on something smooth and cold. Yes: the looking-glass. I slip it into my pocket, hurry to the back door and peer out at the stables. A thin golden line marks the edge of the stable door, still firmly shut.

Good.

Keeping low, I slip down the back stairs into the garden, threading a path between the bean poles and turnip beds, trampling over the collapsed corner of the fence until I arrive at the kitchen door. Here I can see everything, because the door is wide open; light spills through it, engulfing me as I plunge inside.

Of course I step over the empty hole in the floor, trying to ignore Cockeye's blood. Then I head straight for Lady Jane; I'm glad I forgot to release her.

A sip of water should keep her quiet while I move her cage.

'Here you are,' I whisper, dipping a tea cup into the water bucket. The cup fits neatly through the bars and she falls upon it, cackling. I doubt Carver will hear her; I can barely hear Woodbine when she whinnies again.

What else do I need? That chair is too low. That barrel is too heavy. The high stool should do it—but now the hen is fussing, so I lay her on her back and stroke her chest until she's in a trance. She doesn't even stir when I pick up her cage.

Cage, stool, looking glass, gun...I take a deep breath and pray that Gyp is watching over me.

Then I go out.

The only cover between here and the stables is the cool-room. It stands in the beaten expanse of the farmyard like a spar on a beach. I crouch behind it and—Christ, the stench chokes me. It's worse than the hold of the *Lord Lyndoch*. I can't steady my breathing because I don't want to breathe at all.

Now, Tom. *Now.* Quick and quiet. Careful or you might drop something. Lady Jane clucks, but her voice is soft. It's drowned out by Woodbine's frantic whinny, which brings tears to my eyes. I blink them away, averting my gaze from Cockeye's corpse lest the sight of it drains me of courage. Don't look. Stay firm. Step over the blood and brains.

Quietly I set the stool down, hard up against the stable door. Quietly I place the cage on top of it. Quietly I wedge the looking glass between the door and the bars of the cage, within easy reach of the hen.

Then I dash towards the hayloft end of the building, rounding the corner just as Lady Jane starts to peck at the glass. *Tap-tap-tap.* She's high enough to be a human hand.

I cut poor Nugget down earlier, but the rope still hangs from the lift-beam, frayed a little at one end. When I jump to reach it, a sharp pain jabs at my bad knee. My elbow's giving me trouble too as I pull myself up, hand over hand. Normally I'd be shimmying up this rope like a rat on rigging, but it's harder than usual. The gun on my back is as heavy as a cask of wine. My left arm jibs at the weight. Even so, I have to keep going. *Quickly.*

I'll hear the stable door when it opens—those hinges are badly in need of oil, though they've been mute so far. Seems Carver hasn't noticed the hen. Either that or he's lying in wait.

Finally: the lift-beam. My fingers clamp around the wood. I swing my legs up, plant my feet against the edge of the hayloft door and…here I am. Inside at last.

Woodbine's angry snort masks the thud of my landing. Though the hayloft is very dark, there's light beyond the bales in front of me. I squeeze between them, crawling over a carpet of loose hay that muffles my advance, thank God.

I'm flat on my belly when I reach the edge of the hayloft floor. The top of the ladder is just a few inches away. I can't see anything down below—not even the source of the light— but I'd be a fool to lift my head just yet. I have to wait until I hear hinges creak.

I hope I do hear them over the pounding of my heart.

Woodbine is neighing. Rowdy is gasping. *Tap-tap-tap* goes Lady Jane.

Suddenly there's a crash and a yell and a deafening explosion as Carver fires. Lady Jane squawks and flutters.

I rear up and take aim. Carver is by the stable door, which he's just yanked open. The smoking pistol in his right hand is sagging towards the ground. The pistol in his left hand is pointing straight up at the hayloft but his gaze is on the hen flapping around in her broken cage, on the ground by the overturned stool.

Rowdy's the one who spots me first. His eyes widen. The hook in his shoulder is tied to the hook that used to support Mr Barrett's bear trap. Because he's double-ironed, Rowdy can't raise his hands high enough to release himself. He's propped against the wall not far from Woodbine's blood-streaked haunches. His ashen face is shining with sweat or tears (or both). In his good hand he's clutching a pitchfork.

I think I know what Carver's been doing. He's been making Rowdy jab poor Woodbine in the hindquarters. That pitchfork's so long, Rowdy can do it without getting kicked—though he still can't reach Carver.

I don't know what prompts Carver to turn his head. Instinct? The movement of my gun barrel? A change in Rowdy's breathing?

He whips around and fires.

I fire back as his ball whizzes past me.

⊹

My father taught me to shoot. He had a double-barrelled fowling piece that he cherished with all his heart. Every night he would clean it with a flannel soaked in sheep's-foot oil. He told me that cleaning a gun and keeping it dry would stop the barrel from bursting. He showed me how to aim slightly above and in front of a moving target; three inches for every thirty yards of distance, he would say. He made me place my left hand near the ramrod instead of the trigger-guard. He ordered me never to use the gun to beat a bush when I was flushing game. And he stressed the need for calm.

'You must be as cool as a Quaker,' he instructed. 'Don't jerk your head when you fire. Don't close your eyes. Don't pause in your forward movement. If a bird should rise and fly in your face, let it pass you. *Then* you should fire.'

Though my father's temper was on a hair trigger, he was as peaceful as a mill pond when he got behind the barrel of a gun. I've never seen a steadier hand. I once saw him take down a partridge at a hundred yards. For myself, I never equalled him. I never possessed his eye, nor his judgement.

But I am quick. And when presented with a big target, stock still, at a distance of ten yards, my aim is good enough.

That's why I manage to hit Carver.

╫

A red bloom starts to spread across Carver's thigh. He cries out. Even as he crumples, however, he unslings another musket, cocking it one-handed.

I'm ducking when he fires; the shot sends wood-chips spraying down onto my head.

Flat on the floor, I fumble for a new cartridge and tear off its tail. Powder in the pan. Powder in the barrel. Ball. Ramrod.

'Tom!' That's Rowdy's voice, thinner and hoarser than usual. 'He's gone!'

Has he? Or has he got Rowdy at gunpoint?

'Tom, hurry!'

I've finished reloading. One, two…

Three.

When I bob up, I see no sign of Carver. The door stands ajar.

'Tom,' Rowdy quavers. 'I'm sorry I lied to ye, but I had to get away from that bastard…' Even now—shackled, pierced, tied to a hook—he can't seem to stop talking. I slide down the ladder and rush to the door.

'I didn't know what he was plannin' to do, I swear,' Rowdy gabbles. 'He talked about killin' ye for what ye did to him, but I thought they were idle threats. I thought he was headin' north, away from Barrett's farm…'

I slam the door shut. There's a bar, so I use it. Carver can't get back in now.

'Our overseer was workin' us to death or I wouldn't have fallen in with that pair o' damme-boys,' Rowdy continues faintly. 'Ye can't choose yer company on a road gang. Cockeye got us out, and he wouldn't leave without Nobby…'

Quick. Scurrying over to the hook in the wall, I stretch up to flick the loop of rope off it, letting Rowdy slide to the floor with a groan. He drops the bloody pitchfork. His irons are fastened with wire instead of rivets, so I don't even have to use a hammer to get 'em off. Carver left the pliers within easy reach.

'We none of us had guns nor horses nor vittles when

we first escaped.' Rowdy's still rambling on. 'We stole from a few shepherds' huts is all.'

Untwisting the wire on the top-irons takes muscle, but somehow I manage it. The first cuff falls away and I move on to the second one, knowing Rowdy won't have the strength to do it himself.

'Then we found Carver crawlin' around,' he mumbles, 'and he just—well, you've seen what he's like. Told us what to do…wouldn't take no for an answer…Nobby and Cockeye buckled quick enough but I didn't want nothin' to do with him…'

I'm trying not to look at the hook in his shoulder. There's about an inch of it sticking through his shirt.

And that's the second cuff. It hits the floor with a clang.

'I just needed a bed and a bite to eat.' He's whimpering now. 'I'd run away from Carver and I was desperate. He'd walked up to a logger and stuck a knife in his neck—'

'You'd better take that out.' I nod at his shoulder. 'Somewhere away from the horse.'

'Tom—'

'D'you want me to do it?'

He shakes his head, thank God, gasping at the pain it causes him. Then he drags himself across the floor as I slip into the stall next to Woodbine's.

Poor Woodbine. Half a dozen bloody nicks pepper her haunches—but they're not deep. At least Rowdy made sure of that.

When he shrieks, Woodbine tosses her head and I don't blame her. I'm trying not to puke myself.

All right, there's a good girl. I stroke her nose and pat her neck, trying to calm her while Rowdy draws the hook out of his shoulder. I can't help glancing up at the hayloft, though I'm not expecting Carver to appear there. How could he? I put a ball through his leg.

'Done,' Rowdy wheezes. He's the colour of suet, wringing wet and limp with exhaustion, his eyes half-shut. His wound needs binding; the blood's pouring out.

I grab one of the horses' towels, scurry over and drop to my knees beside him. 'Are you fit to ride?' I whisper, pressing the wad of linen to the hole in his shoulder.

Rowdy looks at me, blank-faced. Then he nods.

'He'll be watching that door,' I continue with a jerk of my head. 'He knows the horse can't climb, so he'll be lying in wait just out there.'

Through clenched teeth Rowdy hisses, 'But you shot him!'

'Grazed him.'

'Sure, and he *must* have gone!'

'No.' I rip the sleeve off Rowdy's shirt and use it to tie the towel around his wound. 'As long as he's alive, he'll come for us. He'll want us to pay for his suffering. Wild dogs get more dangerous when they're hurt.'

'Jaysus,' Rowdy moans. His eyes are shut again. 'What'll we do? He took my pistol and cartridges—'

'That's why you need to ride.' I have a plan. Not a great plan, but the only one I can think of. 'If we tarry too long, he'll set the stables on fire,' I explain in a low voice. 'But if we ride out now, together, he'll be waiting for us. That's why we need to distract him.'

'How?'

'I'll tell you.' I take a deep breath, look him in the eye and say, very softly, 'Can you deal with Woodbine on your own?'

'On my…?'

'We have to part.' Before he can do more than stare at me, appalled, I put my mouth to his ear. 'You're not fit to fight, and you're not armed for it,' I breathe. 'But if you can ride out at a gallop, I might hush that murdering cull yet.'

12

I REMEMBER the day Carver first told me he'd killed someone.

It was early evening and I was sitting with Joe in the hut, waiting for my supper. We always took care not to eat before Carver joined us, and Carver hadn't joined us.

'Blacks,' he announced, on finally entering. He had the musket with him because he never let anyone else touch it. Even when Joe was guarding the flock at night, Carver used to sleep with the gun in his bed.

'Where?' said Joe.

'Down by the brook.' Carver sat heavily on the sturdiest stool and grabbed the biggest joint of mutton. 'Don't fret— I scared 'em off.'

No one asked how. Carver told us anyway.

'I showed 'em this.' He fumbled for the leather cord he wore around his neck. I'd never seen what was hanging on the end of it because it was always tucked into his shirt, and when he pulled the thing out, there in the hut, the light was so poor that at first I couldn't make out what it was.

'I showed 'em the gun—and this here—and told 'em not to come back,' he added with a sly grin. His teeth were like the ribs of a wrecked ship in a grey mud-bank. He still had two eyes then, and they both gleamed as he dangled his pendant in front of my nose.

I realised I was looking at an ear, shrunken, shrivelled and sun-scorched. He'd punched a hole in its lobe so that it hung upside down from his leather cord.

'Dried like a raisin in the sun,' he informed me with a touch of pride. He said he'd lopped it off one of the blacks killed on Mr Barrett's first raid, then went on to reminisce about the screams of fleeing women and the excellent marksmanship of Mr Barrett, who had winged several 'coal-black savages' despite the darkness. The pile of corpses they'd left behind, Carver gloated, had been as high as a cow's back. 'A grouse hunt, that one,' he told me. 'You'd have been in your element, Tom Clay, a seasoned poacher like yerself.'

My stomach heaved but I said nothing. I'd been in the hut for barely a week and I already knew I was living with a black-hearted villain.

I understood that my days would be numbered if Carver had anything to do with it.

Peering out of the hayloft, craning my neck like a goose, I can just see the front of the kitchen. There's so much light pouring through its door that the back of Mr Barrett's house is visible too. Carver isn't, though. If he's hiding in either building, he's keeping well away from the windows.

I don't think he's gone that far. If he is hiding, he'll be using the cool-room, which is closer. I wish I had a better view of it from here.

Slinging the carbine over my shoulder, I reach for the lift-beam and hoist myself up and lose my grip and...

God!

No; it's all right. I didn't fall. I lost my hold but the rope was there and I'm safe. I'm good.

Take a deep breath, Tom. Don't falter.

Again I swing myself up—this time I get it right—and manage to squirm along the lift-beam until I reach the gable. Now I can see the cool-room.

But no Carver.

'Carver!' Rowdy yells from beneath me. Muffled by the stable roof, his voice sounds hoarse and a little unsteady; he was so weak that I had to push him up into the saddle. Sitting there with the pitchfork in his right hand and the reins twisted around his left, he looked as if he was going to faint.

But he's found the strength to do his duty.

'Ye might think you've nothing to lose, Dan Carver,' he continues. 'Ye might think, "I can't hang more 'n once, so why not kill two more folk?" But ye should be frettin' on yer immortal soul, my cully.'

I'm hoping the sound of his voice masks the scrape of my feet as I claw my way up onto the stable roof. One side of the roof, fully exposed to the cool-room and kitchen, is bathed in a faint, golden glow from the kitchen door. But the other side is in shadow, so I heave myself up there, clinging to the roof-ridge with my fingertips.

Rowdy's still talking.

'Now, I don't know if you're a religious man,' he says to Carver, 'but there's not a soul on earth can be sure what awaits him when he dies. And what if killing us gets you twenty more years in purgatory? Assuming, o' course, that you don't go straight to hell...'

My cheek is pressed flat against the wooden shingles. Slowly, cautiously, I raise my head and peer over the roof-ridge.

I spot Carver at once. His musket barrel is poking out from behind the cool-room. He's readying himself.

'What'll ye lose by lettin' us live?' Rowdy demands, straining to keep some vigour in his speech. 'By the time we get to town, you'll be well away. And it's us who'll probably hang for this, not you. After all, who's goin' to listen to a couple o' lags ridin' their master's horse?'

I adjust my position and raise the carbine until its muzzle is trained on Carver's gun. Then I reach into my pocket, pull out Mr Barrett's pliers and let 'em slide down the front of the roof.

Bump-bump-bump-CLANG.

Carver thrusts his head out from behind the cool-room. He looks up and fires.

I duck as the stable door crashes open.

When I lift my head again, I spy Rowdy: he's swerved to the left and is riding towards the road. He kicks poor Woodbine into a gallop and she gamely hurls herself forward, though the holes in her rump must hurt like hell.

Carver drops the musket and raises a pistol. In his quest for a clear shot, he's stumbled out from his hiding place.

Now. *Now.* I fire at him before he can fire at Rowdy.

There's a spray of dust. God dammit! My only chance and I missed!

Carver jerks back behind the cool-room. He's gone to ground and I'll have to lure him out again. I duck back behind the roof-ridge to reload.

One more shot. I've only one more shot.

Carver fires his second musket: flash in the pan. He curses.

The darkness has swallowed Rowdy, though I can still hear Woodbine's fading hoof-beats. She's escaped. She's saved him.

Now I have to save myself.

Slowly, Tom; don't drop anything. Powder in the pan. Powder in the muzzle.

Before I can pull the trigger, Carver's pistol-ball hits the roof and I shy from the impact. That's three shots. One more and he'll be stopping to load his weapons.

'I ate a native bear once,' he growls. Is he talking to me? Is he still by the cool-room? I can't tell.

Three pokes of the ramrod. Replace the ramrod. Half-cock

the hammer. Now—where is he? I push the gun barrel cautiously back over the roof-ridge.

Nothing.

Inch by inch I raise my head…

A shingle fractures nearby. Four shots—that's it.

In one easy movement I thrust myself up over the roof-ridge and aim my carbine. There he is, stumbling towards the hayloft end of the stables, dragging that left leg, which is wrapped in a torn and bloody strip of cloth. His gaze lifts. His hand rises. There's a pistol in it—

He fires wide as he limps along, and I duck back down. Curse it, he's reloaded.

'The bear was up a tree and I threw rocks at it until it fell.' He's moving towards the hayloft door. His voice tells me as much.

I uncock the carbine, sling it over my shoulder and start sliding back the way I came. The roof's quite steep and, though I'm not exactly hanging by my fingertips, they're doing a lot of the work.

'Then I cut off its head and skinned it and pulled its guts out,' Carver's directly under the hayloft, now, and I'm directly above it. But is he pressed against the wall? Are the eaves sheltering him? Is he reloading?

I won't know until I look.

If Gyp were here, she could take him down from behind. Please, Gyp, I know you're up in Heaven with the angels. Don't let this bastard kill me.

The hammer clicks as I cock it.

Go.

I stick my head out over the eaves, manoeuvring the carbine as best I can. The angle's bad. I'd be firing one-handed, and Carver's lurking in such dense shadow that I can barely make out his silhouette. He's blurring into the darkness of the wall.

That scratching sound is a ramrod being jabbed into a muzzle. He'll have his pistol loaded in a second or two.

I can't waste my last shot. If I don't fire now, will Carver know I've only a single ball? Or will he think I've nothing left?

He might expose himself if he feels there's no risk in it.

'But let me tell you summat, Tom Clay,' he says hoarsely. 'I'm going to pull your guts out before I cut off yer head.'

What's he doing, loading another gun? Unless I'm mistook, I just heard the crinkle of cartridge paper. He must have realised that he's safe down there, in the shelter of the eaves, as long as I'm up here. He must be making good use of the time he's gained.

'And then I'm going to cut off both yer ears,' Carver concludes, 'and add 'em to my collection.'

God ha' mercy, he's heading round the back. From there he can step out from under the eaves and see me plastered against the shingles like a fly squashed on a whitewashed wall.

With a thump and a clatter, I throw my leg over the roof-ridge and heave myself onto the other side of the roof.

Carver suddenly fires. A ball whizzes past. He must have seen a flurry of limbs against the starry sky.

'Like shooting a bear up a tree.' He's on the move again. Gravel crunches unevenly; he's limping, his pace slow. That's where I have the advantage...

Yes, he's retracing his steps. Coming round the front, by the sound of it. There—he's put some distance between himself and the stables, so he has a clear shot at the roof.

But not at me. Even as he raises his musket, I scramble back over the roof-ridge.

He shoots. Misses.

My cheek slams down onto the shingles and I'm hanging by one hand; the other's clamped to my carbine. He'll come back around for another shot, from the rear. Or maybe that's what he's hoping I'll think.

What if he tricks me?

Time I became the hunter instead of the game. Time I took the lead.

He's over there, tracing a wide half-circle around the hayloft, well away from the eaves. That means I'll have a clean shot if I can just get close enough to the edge of the roof. I'll be more exposed, but so will he. And I'm a deal more spry.

The carbine goes back over my shoulder. Sliding along the roof, I'm close to the lift-beam when I spot him. He's a good twenty yards away, hobbling along, his head turned towards me.

Can he see me, though? He doesn't fire. He has the light from the kitchen at his back and I'm on the dark side of the roof. This is it. I have the advantage.

I drag the gun off my shoulder. Brace my feet against the shingles. Release the roof-ridge so I can line up my shot and—

My feet start to slip. I grab the ridge-cap again, unthinking. That's when I drop the gun.

My father was a great one for coursing hares. His lurcher, Morton, had the finest nose I ever knew in a dog, and a good turn of speed as well. But my brother had a sighthound, a whippet named Switch, who won more bets than any other dog in the county. He was the king of coursers, quick and cunning and fearless, though not good with a quarry that didn't bolt. When a hare or rabbit had the sense to keep still, Switch was inclined to overlook it. That's why he coursed with Morton, who could sniff out anything, anywhere. No nettle patch or lavender bush could protect a hare from Morton.

One day I saw the two dogs flush a hare who sprang five feet into the air, straight over Morton's back. There followed a hundred-yard stretch, then so many turns and ricks and curves and wrenches that the dogs lost their advantage. The hare went this way, that way, this way and that; she dodged and zig-zagged, swerved and jumped, and wouldn't let herself be driven. Morton was already tiring when she reached cover. Neither he nor Switch ever caught that hare.

I think of her now, fleetingly, as I cling to the roof-ridge.

✢

My carbine skates down the roof and lands on the ground with a thud and a rattle. Carver freezes for an instant. Then he changes tack, stumbling straight towards me, making for the wall beneath the hayloft.

He must think I'm on the ground myself—that I just slipped off the roof.

I might have a minute's grace while he flattens himself against the wall, inches towards the nor'west corner, cocks his gun, prepares to shoot and—then what? When he peers behind the stables, he'll see I'm not there. He mightn't see the carbine, at first; there's grass out the back that hasn't been grazed in a while.

As quietly as possible I slither over the roof-ridge and hang for moment, turning my head to peer at the kitchen and cool-room behind me. Then I let go of the ridge-cap and slide down the roof, which isn't so steep that I fly off it. Instead I grab the eaves with both hands. From there I can lower myself, very carefully, until...

Damn it. Even with my arms stretched almost out of their sockets, my feet are still dangling at least five feet off the ground.

Please, God—*please, Gyp*—I count to three and drop.

The impact jars every bone in my body. I've hurt my foot and I've no gun and I made a noise when I landed. Did Carver hear me?

I can hear him. He's coming; his lumbering footsteps are heading this way. Mine are lighter, softer, but what if he follows my tracks? I'm not going to make it—not all the way to the kitchen. And even if I do, how will it help me? A boning knife is no match for a loaded gun.

If I lock myself in, he'll set fire to the roof. He's done it before.

I have to hide. Not behind the cool-room; inside it. You'd have to be a madman to go in there. Holding my breath, I push open the cool-room door a few inches. One or two chilled flies stir, then settle. There are no windows. The room is pitch black and when I close the door behind me, I might as well be in a coal-mine.

At least I can't see what's in here. And when I pinch my nostrils shut, I can't smell it either. I'll be able to feel it, though. Groping my way forward is the bravest thing I've ever done. One step. Two…

The toe of my boot sinks into something soft. I swallow hard, stretch out my hand and hunker down. My fingers hit a clothed joint—a knee or an elbow. Probably an elbow. Which is attached to a shoulder, which disappears under… what's this? A leg?

God ha' mercy. They're stacked in a pile.

I pat my way up…and up…past a head of hair and a dangling hand and a boot and an ear and the flies scatter and my guts flip and I'm going to puke but I can't, he'll smell it, hear it. *I mustn't be sick.*

The pile of corpses is nearly as tall as I am. I don't know who's on top; I don't want to know. Can I hide behind the pile? He'll find me there if he comes in to check. But if I crawl under it, I might be safe.

I can't. It would kill me.

But Carver will kill me if I don't.

Oh God, God, God.

I feel my way around the pile until I'm as far from the door as I can get. Then I drop to my hands and knees, facing the wall, and push my feet between the floor and…something. Feels like a ribcage.

The pile shifts but doesn't topple. Everyone in it is solid

and weighty; Mrs Trumble was almost fat. But I'm just skin and bone. I don't disturb the others too much as I wriggle beneath 'em. The worst thing is the noise—a sigh here, a gurgle there. Corpses have a lot of gas in 'em and when the pressure shifts, so does the gas.

Our Father, who art in heaven, hallowed be thy name. Thy kingdom come, thy will be done, in earth as it is in heaven...

The flies drone about, bumping into me. An arm flops down. A body slides. I keep going, squirming my way backwards, deeper and deeper, until only my head is sticking out. I can't go any further. But Mrs Trumble's petticoat is draped over my face, so Carver won't see me. Why would he want to go searching under Mrs Trumble's petticoat?

He's taking his time. Perhaps he's checking in the stables. Perhaps he's searching the hayloft. I can feel something crawling across my chin. Pray God that's not a maggot.

My mind flashes to Carver's account of Mr Barrett's raid, and the pile of bodies Mr Barrett left behind. Carver gloried in that pile; I could see his eyes light up, hear the relish in his voice when he described it to me. Has he tried to build it again here in the cool-room? Has he been thinking on it for too long?

I'm holding my breath, now. I'm holding my nose. I'm straining my ears.

And here he is.

Hinges creak as the door opens. A faint wash of light glints on a grey fingernail not six inches from my nose.

'*Whoof!*' says Carver. He gags, then begins to cough. 'Christ, you'd have to be desperate.'

171

He cocks his gun: click. His heels scrape against the dirt floor. One step. Two steps. 'But o' course, you *are* desperate,' he says, almost choking on the words.

He knows. He knows I'm here. *How can he know I'm here?*

'If you like the company o' the dead so much, Tom Clay,' he growls, 'then why don't you join 'em?'

He can't see me. Can he? I clench my teeth, screw up my eyes and—

He fires.

The noise sounds like a thunderbolt in this tiny hut. My ears ring. When the bodies above me quiver, I realise what he's done.

He shot 'em. He fired straight into the people he already killed.

But the bullet didn't pass through.

Another shot. And another. Above me, Charlie and Jim and the Trumbles are blocking every ball he can pump into 'em.

Forgive us our trespasses, as we forgive them who trespass against us...

13

THE GAOL at Bury was like a wheel. At its centre was the governor's house, which had eight sides. Each side overlooked a yard, and the walls between the yards were the spokes of the wheel. Where the walls ended, the rim began; there were common rooms below and sleeping cells above—two levels of 'em—all with windows that faced the governor's house.

So there were no private corners in that prison. The governor seemed always to be watching, even when he wasn't. I never felt safe from prying eyes, or from the threat of sudden punishment. I remember trying to find a place in the yard where I couldn't be seen, but no such place existed. The governor's house was three storeys high, with a flat roof.

He used to pace around that roof like a guard atop a castle tower, peering down at us.

I remember the sensation as I lie cowering in the cool-room, waiting for Carver's eye to fall on me.

⧺

Carver's angry. He's breathing through his teeth, hissing like a snake. His dragging step slowly circles the pile of bodies. Paper rips. A ball rolls down a barrel.

He must be reloading.

Then he stops. There's a pause, followed by a jangling noise that puzzles me. All at once I remember the butcher's hooks chained to the rafters. Mr Barrett used to hang his mutton in here to age.

Something buries itself with a meaty thunk in the topmost cadaver.

'Christ, but you're going to pay for this, boy,' Carver growls.

The weight above me begins to shift. Carver grunts and gasps as he slowly, painfully, skewers a corpse and hauls it off the pile. It rolls to the ground. The impact jars every tooth in my head.

A scuffle and a thud are followed by a short, sharp cry. Carver's hurt himself.

He must be in pain. He must have lost so much blood. Why doesn't he just *lie down and die*? The bastard's strong as a bullock.

'Well, well, if it ain't Mr Barrett,' he says, with another thrust of the hook. 'Not so high and mighty now, are we?'

174

I clap my hand over my mouth, swallowing down the bile that's rising in my throat. Mr Barrett. Mr Barrett's up there. He was no saint, but he was no Carver. He had a wife. He had a pack of fine dogs.

He hits the ground and a foul smell engulfs me, making my eyes water and my stomach churn.

'Whoof!' says Carver again. 'Not too sweet, neither, eh?'

I can feel the impact when his hook snags the next corpse. He tugs and strains and heaves. All at once my burden grows lighter as another body joins Mr Barrett's. That's three in total. Then number four slams down.

Only two more left. Any minute now, Carver's going to see me. He's going to see me and he's going to kill me. But at least I'll be with Ma again. And Gyp. Oh God, if only Gyp were here.

'Well, now, 'tis none other than Lottie Trumble,' Carver gloats. 'Greedy old bitch. You know what she tried to do, once? Tried to gimme a plate o' gristle. Looked me straight in the eye and claimed 'twas good meat.' He snorts. 'Hah! I know good meat from bad, fusty-luggs, and you're bad meat now, my blowen.'

In goes the hook. Mrs Trumble's petticoat begins to slide over my scalp as Carver drags her heavy form off her husband's. I feel cool air on the top of my head. He'll see me now. He's going to—

'There you are!'

Please God, make it quick. Make the shot clean.

'Shaking like a whipped dog,' he says. 'If you hadn't winged me, Tom Clay, I'd be jumping on Trumble's back, squashing you like a rotten apple. But I don't have the full use o' me limbs.'

He leans closer. Craning around to squint up at him, I can just make out the glint of his teeth and his one, glaring eye. The hook in his right hand is twitching like a cat's tail. He's waving a pistol in his left.

'I could bury this hook in yer skull,' he continues, 'but there'd be no fun in that. I think I'll start with the belly, just as soon as I get George Trumble off you, and—'

Thunk.

That's not the hook.

Carver howls and reels away from me. As I pull myself out from beneath George Trumble, I glimpse a shadow in the doorway, yanking the tips of a pitchfork out of Carver's back.

Rowdy?

Carver fires wildly over his own shoulder, then spins around until he's facing the door. He's dropped the hook. I hear it hit the ground.

This is my chance.

I dart forward to grab the hook while Carver totters like a half-felled tree, making noises like a cross-saw. The pistol falls from his hand. Gun smoke burns my nostrils.

Rowdy stumbles backwards a few steps and keels over onto the dirt, but Carver doesn't fall. Somehow he manages to stay upright, swaying and staggering across the threshold. He drags a musket off his punctured back, screeching in pain, and points it at Rowdy.

That's when I swing the butcher's hook.

It digs deep into Carver's shoulder, just above the four bloody holes in his coat. He's jerked backwards. His musket tips up and fires into the air.

That was his last shot—because he doesn't have my carbine, thank God. But he's quick enough to slam the butt of his musket back into my chest and it's like the kick of a horse; it sends me flying. I land on top of Mr Barrett as Carver wrenches the hook from his body and turns to confront me. He's bleeding and bellowing, wild as a bull in a butcher's yard. He drives the gun-butt towards my head.

I roll aside and jump to my feet. The butt hits the floor, then rests there a moment as Carver leans on the musket, dizzy with pain. I fling myself at the pitchfork, which is lying on the ground not far from where Rowdy's landed. Scooping it up, I turn to see the wavering muzzle of Carver's second musket, pointing straight at me.

Time seems to stand still as I watch him pull the trigger, then—

Nothing happens. The gun isn't loaded.

I bat it aside with the pitchfork. He sweeps the stock around and whacks me on the side of the jaw. I drop to one knee, my head ringing, my arms swinging. The pitchfork handle connects with his wounded leg, which buckles under the impact. Suddenly we're both on our hands and knees, face to face in the dimness.

For an instant we stare at each other, gulping down air. I raise the pitchfork. He drives his gun at my head. I duck. He roars. I lunge. He slams into me and throws a punch that connects with my nose. But when I fall back, yelping, he doesn't try to hit me again.

Instead he lurches to his feet and staggers away, dripping blood, bent double, lame, breathless, weaving like a drunkard and leaning on his gun.

The pistol. He dropped it.

I crawl back into the cool-room and grope around in the dirt until my fingers close on the butt of the pistol. Blood dribbles from my nose and mouth as I grab the door-jamb and pull myself up. I'm dizzy. My chest hurts. My ears are ringing. I can hardly stand.

I'm alive, though. And Carver...Carver looks to be at death's door.

He's heading for the southern paddock. Peering around the side of the cool-room, I catch sight of his dark, misshapen bulk floundering into the night, leaving a trail of blood. I should go after him now, while he's weak. Before he reloads. I should fetch my carbine from behind the stables and kill him with my very last ball.

But I'm seeing double. It hurts to breathe. My knees feel like skeins of wool.

And there's Rowdy...

I turn to look at him. Don't tell me he's been shot. Did Carver shoot him?

'Rowdy?'

He's flat on his back. His eyes are closed. His dark curls are spread out around a face so pale it seems to glow in the moonlight. The towel I tied to his shoulder is drenched in blood.

Powder-marks stipple his forehead—but I can't see any wounds.

'Rowdy!'

I squat down and start feeling for the path of a pistol-ball. There's no blood in his hair. There's blood on his shirt, but the stains are dry as chalk. So is the blood on his hands. He can't have been shot—unless the ball passed through the hole in his shoulder? The towel I tied there is wet and warm, but not ripped to shreds...

He can't have been shot.

'Wake up. Please.' I pat his cheek. Has he fainted? He must have fainted. He's lost so much blood, and Carver nearly winged him, and the pain must be terrible...

But he came back. I didn't think he would. I didn't think he'd have the strength. I sent him away and he came straight back.

He came back and saved me.

'Please,' I tell him, with a catch in my throat. 'Don't die.' Glancing over my shoulder, I check that Carver isn't anywhere near. Then I lean close to Rowdy's ear and whisper, 'I'm just fetching my gun. I'll not be long. I haven't left you.'

That's when his eyelids flutter open.

Thank God. 'Can you hear me?' I ask. That shot by his temple would have all but deafened him.

'Tom,' he croaks.

'I'm here.' Dropping the pistol, I take his hand and squeeze it.

'Carver...'

'He's gone. For now.'

A crooked smile cracks across his face as he mutters, 'Sure, and ye saw him off. You're a warrior, indeed.'

'No, you saw him off. You saved me.' Tears sting my eyes. 'You—you came back...'

''Course I did.' He gasps and winces, as if from a stabbing pain. When he continues, his voice is tight with it. 'I'll have ye know I'm as good a man as Gyp.'

I know. I can see that now. You came back for me.

'I have to fetch my gun,' I warn him. 'Stay here. Don't move. Play dead. He'll not shoot you if he thinks you're dead.'

'Mmmm,' Rowdy grunts. He shuts his eyes again.

'I'll fetch the gun and put you in the house.' There are beds in the house. There are fireplaces. There's laudanum and clean linen and glass in the windows, to keep out the flies. 'I won't leave you, I swear.'

Rowdy doesn't answer. He's playing dead. He *looks* dead. But I can feel the pulse still beating, very weakly, in his wrist.

So I lay his hand carefully across his breast before I struggle to my feet and limp towards the stables.

⟶⟵

My mother used to tell me Cornish tales every night before I went to sleep. She would hold me in her lap, by the fire, with her chin on my hair and her eyes on the flames, and she would murmur stories that she'd heard when she was a little girl in Cornwall. Sometimes she would sing to me. Sometimes she would rock me back and forth, stroking my head. But mostly she told me her tales.

She told me that ants were faeries in the very last stage of their life on earth. She told me about a giant who used to come out of his seaside cavern, sink ships by throwing stones at them, and eat the sailors he brought back home.

She also told me that a married giant named Bolster once fell in love with St Agnes. The saint asked him to prove his devotion by filling a hole in the ground with his blood. It was a small hole and he was a big giant, so he opened a vein over the hole. But what he didn't know was that the hole led down to the sea—so his blood kept flowing until he died.

I think of that tale as I help Rowdy all the way across the yard, up the back stairs, into Mr Barrett's bedroom. I have to hold him up like a crutch, and every step opens his wound again, causing fresh blood to flow. How much more blood can he spare? Though a fine, big man, he's underweight, and must be near emptied.

At least he's been bled, I suppose. Bleeding helps to bring down fevers.

'Don't move again,' I tell him, as he collapses onto Mr Barrett's feather bed. 'I'll fetch some water. And there's laudanum here, for the pain.' There are spare shirts, too. Rowdy's already stolen one, so we might as well take another. 'I'll dress that wound again when I come back.'

'A drop o' the craither wouldn't go amiss,' Rowdy groans.

'Yes…well…I'll look.' Is it wise to mix rum and laudanum? I don't know. Besides, I'm sure Carver would have drunk all the booze in the house.

But before I go searching for Mr Barrett's brandy bottle, there's something else I have to do.

The *Lord Lyndoch* was a sickly ship. We'd barely left port before smallpox broke out; Mr Pineo, the surgeon superintendent, had to go about vaccinating those who hadn't already been infected. Then two men died of consumption. Then, after we passed the Cape of Good Hope, half the ship was laid low with scurvy. Mr Pineo didn't have berths enough in his hospital. He was so busy that he needed more attendants. And he was blind enough to put his faith in Obadiah Johnson.

Johnson was a shuffling rogue. As a forger, he was greatly favoured; all the lettered lags were. When Mr Pineo gave him lemon-juice duty, Johnson used it to his own advantage, withholding the cure from any young lag who wouldn't stoop to be his molly.

Two of 'em took their concerns to Mr Pineo, who referred 'em to Mr Stead, the master. But nothing happened because Mr Stead thought Mr Pineo conceited and Mr Pineo thought Mr Stead dishonest. As far as I could tell, they were both right. Mr Pineo, a naval man, was always trying to teach the merchant crew their business, while Mr Stead was skimming supplies. I know this after seeing the volume of stores he unloaded for sale when we reached Sydney Cove. There's a reason ten men died of scurvy on that voyage.

Scurvy is an ugly affliction, and it filled us all with terror. So did the flogging that one lad received for stabbing Johnson with a sharpened spoon handle. Johnson's wound wasn't bad, but the flogging was. Mr Stead chose to regard the attack as mutinous, and after that, Johnson had free rein. Many preferred his attentions to the blight of cankered gums and lost teeth, having already endured worse buggery aboard the prison hulks, but I wasn't among these unhappy souls.

That's why I spent the last three weeks of the voyage in a hospital berth. I could hardly lift a hand to defend myself, but Johnson's only revenge was to leave me alone. Some days I wasn't fed at all. Sometimes the food was left beside me, and the lag in the next bed stole it.

I survived only because the crewman given the task of killing the ship's rats after I fell ill would come to me for advice. In exchange he'd give me food and water and other small attentions.

I'll never forget how it felt to be marooned in that bed, too weak to rise and too ill to do more than groan. I don't want Rowdy to feel like that. I won't leave him for long if I can help it.

I couldn't save Gyp, but I'm not going to let Rowdy die.

⫟

My father turns to me in the dark. He's angry; I can hear it in his breathing. He raises his hand and there's a riding crop in it.

'No, Pa, please—'

I gasp as I'm jolted awake, wide-eyed. This isn't my father's cottage, nor the shepherds' hut, neither. I'm not even lying down. I'm in a chair—a padded chair—with a carbine across my lap.

I'm in Mr Barrett's bedroom.

It must be morning, because daylight is flooding through the strip of exposed window-glass that I wasn't able to cover last night. The rest of the window is blocked by Mr Barrett's campaign chest, and by the barrel sitting on top of it. The fireplace is blocked, too; I packed it full of pots and firewood and sharp tools before I went to sleep.

Somewhere a cock is crowing. Could even one of the chickens have survived the night?

Rowdy did. His eyes are open. He's lying on Mr Barrett's bed, under Mr Barrett's bedclothes, wearing Mr Barrett's shirt. Mr Barrett's card table sits beside him, its top cluttered with an empty glass, a dirty plate, a heel of bread, a joint of mutton, the vial of laudanum, a bloody cloth and Mr Barrett's duelling pistol.

'Good morning,' Rowdy says in a weak voice.

I sit up, blinking and rubbing my eyes. My head aches, my nose is still throbbing and my foot isn't quite what it should be, but I'm well enough.

'I see ye cleaned yerself up,' says Rowdy.

I did that. You could smell me a mile off, and a stench won't help me while I'm stalking, for all I might stay downwind. A little soap, a little water, new slops from the laundry—the only thing I need now are a few handfuls of crushed leaves and damp earth, to rub into my boot-soles.

Rising, I go to the door, open it cautiously and peer out. Mr Barrett's four dog traps are lying on the floor of the hallway, carefully spaced, between the bedroom and the front door. I've scattered a carpet of broken bottles around 'em.

But the path to the back door is clear.

'He'll not bother us again,' Rowdy says behind me. 'He's probably dead by now.'

Hah! I pull my head back and turn to look at Rowdy. He's not so handsome anymore. His colour is muddy and there are dark circles around his eyes. His cheeks are sunk and his hair is clinging damply to his skull. He looks bad. He looks like the fellow at Bury gaol who was kicked half to death by a turnkey in his cell.

'That's what Joe and I thought last time,' I point out. 'But we made a mistake.' Shouldering my carbine, I add grimly, 'This time I have to be sure.'

Rowdy's eyes widen in alarm. He struggles to sit up but the pain of it defeats him and he sinks into the pillows again. 'No, lad, please,' he croaks. 'Don't even think of it. That Carver—he's mad. He's a wild beast—'

'My pa was no better. But he didn't kill me.' Seeing Rowdy's expression, I remember how I used to feel whenever I left Gyp outside the hut at night. So I approach the bed and lay a hand on Rowdy's arm. 'You'll be safe,' I assure him. 'Just don't leave. Don't use them back stairs.'

'Tom—'

'Carver won't get in here. No one will. I've made sure of that.' It occurs to me suddenly that I need to eat, so I pick up the bread and bite off a mouthful as hard and dry as free-stone. 'Even if someone does get in, you'll have the pistol. Who's going to know it isn't loaded?'

'Tom—listen.' Rowdy gropes for my hand. 'You should take the horse. You should ride for town.'

'Where *is* the horse?' I ask, pulling away. Rowdy looks surprised.

'Couldn't you find her?' he says.

'I didn't search for her.' I was a mite busy last night, what with laying traps, fetching meat, binding wounds and fortifying the bedroom. 'Why—what did you do with her?' A terrible thought strikes me. 'She's not dead?'

'Ah, no, she's good.' His speech is slowing, as if he's too tired to talk. I don't like the way he's slurring his words. There were lags in hospital aboard the *Lord Lyndoch* who did the same, and it was never a good sign. 'She's a quarter-hour's walk down the road, in a meadow. You can't miss her.'

The meadow. I know the meadow. Carver knows the meadow, too. But he was heading in the opposite direction last night, when he stumbled off. Would he have had the strength to go looking for Woodbine? He'd have known she was close, because Rowdy came back.

Rowdy came back before Carver could kill me.

'Tom.' With his last flicker of strength, Rowdy raises his hand to grab at my coat-tails as I'm turning away. 'Don't go chasin' Carver. Sure, and no good'll come of it.'

Gently I detach myself. 'If I don't go after him, he'll come after me,' I point out, heading for the door.

'Please, Tom.'

I pause on the threshold. 'If you're worried, go to Gyp's grave and hide there. But *don't tread on the middle step outside.* Remember that.'

I'm not sure what else to say. That I shan't fail him? That he mustn't lose hope?

'You should take the horse into town,' he says. 'Tell 'em what happened. Tell 'em to send the troopers.'

And leave you here, alone, unarmed, with only a few dog-traps standing between you and Carver?

Not likely.

'If ye ride into town, and tell the troopers what befell Barrett's farm, like as not they'll believe ye,' Rowdy wheezes. 'Sure, and you're a slip of a thing—I could blow you away with a breath. 'Twill be hard for folk to believe that ye killed nine people.'

'Rowdy—'

'I'm not finished! Fact is, I'm destined for the triangle—or worse—because I bolted. Stay with me and ye'll be punished for consortin' with an escaped convict.' He offers me his crooked smile. His lips are dry and cracked. 'You go. Take the horse. I don't want to spoil yer chances.'

I shake my head. 'No.'

'Tom—'

'No.' He's talking pap. 'If I go to town I'll be hanged for murder. The troopers won't believe me. There's not a magistrate in the colony will think I'm innocent.'

'Lad, if ye could see yer own face—you've the face of a choirboy—'

'*I can't talk like you!*' God ha' mercy, we've no time for this. 'I've never passed false coin in pubs. I've not the knack of persuading folk.' But I have to persuade Rowdy, so I put everything I've got into it, trying not to pause or stammer. 'Once I've dealt with Carver, we can lay our plans. I've lived off the land for weeks, in England, and know the way of it—even in a strange country. If we fight shy o' the blacks, and mind how we light our fires, we'll fare well enough.'

'Tom—'

'Most bolters are caught because they don't know how to feed themselves. They steal and plunder. We shan't.' Seeing his quizzical look, I stand my ground.

'We cannot part. We'll fail if we do.' I don't say that he's the only true friend I've ever had, leaving aside my dogs. I don't say that I need a friend to help me survive the dreams that plague me every night. All I say is, 'Rest here. I'll not desert you. Don't you desert me.'

'Lad—'

'Stay quiet,' I add. Then I head down the hallway.

'He'll kill ye…' Rowdy calls, his voice cracking.

No he won't. Not if I kill him first.

Outside, the air is fresh and the sky overcast. Colonel Bates the rooster is scratching in the dirt. The kitchen chimney isn't smoking.

There's no sign of Carver—or of anyone else. I can smell the cool-room from way over here. Those poor folk need burying. I'll do it when I return.

Three wooden steps lead from the garden to the back veranda. I jump to the ground from the top step and study the next one down. It looks convincing enough, though I put it there myself last night, after removing the original stair-tread. What rests on the risers now is a rotten piece of wood as fragile as a biscuit. When I lift it up, chips and flakes of wood patter down onto the open bear trap underneath.

The jaws of this trap are still stained with Cockeye's blood. I had to pull 'em off his ankle, last night, using the clamp and the poker. 'Twas harder than entering a pitch-black cool-room full of corpses.

Cockeye's in the cool-room now, along with the rest of 'em. I owed him that much. And I'll bury him too, when I come back. If I come back.

Carefully I lower the rotten plank. Carefully I sweep away all the loose splinters. Then I make for the kitchen, where there's water and cheese and meat.

I don't want my belly growling while I'm sitting in a covert, stalking game.

⧺

A week after Joe and I first crippled Dan Carver, a pack of dogs attacked the fold. Three of 'em kept Gyp and Pedlar occupied, while a fourth squeezed under a hurdle before Joe could stop it. Once in the fold, this beast was protected from musket balls because Joe couldn't shoot for fear of hitting a sheep. The big grey bastard ran through the flock, taking a bite out of every sheep it passed—ten in all. Only three of 'em recovered.

I remember how I threw myself in front of Sweet-pea to shield her. I remember how I stood fast, armed with nothing but my lantern, and yelled at the approaching dog. I was so angry I would gladly have sunk my own teeth into its neck. I would have done anything to guard my sheep, which were so frightened they rushed the fence, almost overturning it.

The wild dog must have sensed my anger because it made no move against me. Instead it veered and fled, and was pursued as far as the tree-line by Gyp, who savaged it cruelly before they parted. Poor Gyp suffered a torn ear, but I was untouched.

Later it occurred to me that I could have had my throat torn out or my limbs worried. Joe realised it too. 'The good shepherd giveth his life for the sheep,' he recited, then muttered that I was a fool.

But I don't think it foolish to defend those whom God has seen fit to place in my care. What is a shepherd if not the protector of his sheep? And I'm still a shepherd, though my flock is much reduced.

I might have failed Sweet-pea, and Mags, and Daisy, and Queenie, and Nell. But I'm not going to fail Rowdy Cavanagh.

14

A POACHER who has a good dog can grow lazy. My father told me that. He used to take me stalking without the dogs. My brother would come too. We would follow a hind to its couch, or a hare to its nest, by relying wholly on our eyes and ears and noses. We would watch for prints, droppings and tufts of fur. If we didn't, my father would beat us.

Sometimes, when I hid from his fierce temper, he would try to track me too. He couldn't, though, not without his dog. I grew cunning and had a knack for hiding in plain sight. At Bury gaol, though constantly watched, I never really caught the turnkey's eye. Other folk were put on the treadmill or had their food and bedding stolen, but I always avoided notice. Since I had no money for the luxuries many inmates bought, there was nothing of interest in my possession. Still, I like to think that my talent for concealment worked to my advantage.

On the voyage to New South Wales I skulked about like the rats I killed. A ship such as the *Lord Lyndoch* has any number of dark holes and dim corners, because the convict quarters are never lit. Among all those hundreds of government men, I was small and quick and quiet and noticed only when the indents were checked for someone with a poacher's skills. Mostly I went unregarded—except by Obadiah Johnson, who had a finely trained eye for the insignificant.

I'm hoping I'll go unregarded now. I'm hoping Dan Carver will be as oblivious to me as the eels and the trout and the pheasants were back in Suffolk.

As a hunter, you have to be quieter than your prey.

+++

Dan Carver's blood trail begins at the door of the cool-room. From there it runs past the kitchen, around the back of my old sleeping quarters and into the southern paddock.

As soon as I hit the long grass, I get down and start to crawl in case Carver is hiding in the forest with his gun trained on me. Besides, keeping low makes it easier to track blood-spots on the ground or smears of blood on the grass. If Gyp were here, I wouldn't have to be so canny. Without Gyp's nose, I have to rely on my eyes and ears.

I can't rely on my nose, because I'm pinching it shut. Poor Buttercup has been lying in the paddock for at least two days now, and badly needs burying. She's left her pats all over the place, too, and they don't smell too sweet when your face is a foot off the ground.

There are other leavings in the grass, as well. Kangaroo pellets. Bird droppings. Fresh dog turds. No doubt the wild dogs have been feeding on Buttercup and scouring the farm for loose chickens.

I'm glad I shut the door to the cool-room.

Here's the edge of the paddock. The grass thins; the shade thickens; the tree trunks rear up from a bed of matted roots. The forest is so dense that there's not much underbrush. I can read the blood trail on the dry earth as clear as ink-marks on paper: one spot, two spots, veering off to the east.

Carver was dragging his leg as he walked. He paused here for a while and left a dense spatter of droplets before moving on. That's the mark of a gun-butt in the soil, cut deep. He must have been leaning on his musket.

He had to weave around this rock because he didn't have the strength to step over it. He had to skirt this bush because he didn't have the strength to push through it. This is where he fell and got up again. This is where he stopped to reload a gun. There's black powder on the ground and a torn strip of paper.

What a fool.

The drops of blood are more widely spaced now; by this time his bleeding must have slowed. But it doesn't matter. A big man like Carver, made clumsy by pain—I don't need a blood trail to see where he went. He left a bloody hand-print on that tree trunk. And over there, in the distance, he left a loose thread on a thorny branch.

When I reach the thread I can see it has blood on it. What now? He hit a dense thicket too wide to bypass, so he had to forge straight through. There are snapped twigs everywhere. Trampled leaves. Crushed branches. He's cut a path for me, all the way to the other side.

Above my head, a little thorn-beak cries out as I pass. I look up to see it flit from tree to tree, piping out its alarm.

'Shh!' I tell it, but there's no calming one of those birds when you're in its domain. All I can do is move on through the scrub, hoping Carver isn't anywhere nearby.

I have a strong feeling somebody is. Time and again, my skin prickles—but when I turn, there's no one. It could be the forest. Or a ghost. Or…

Pray God I'm not being stalked by a black.

Suddenly there's a break in the canopy. Mottled sunshine glints on a narrow, rocky riverbed lined with tumbled boulders. I cower behind a tree trunk and scan the open ground, my gun raised and half-cocked. Carver's been here—there are signs—but he doesn't seem to be here anymore. I certainly can't see him.

Cautiously I advance into the open, the muzzle of my carbine sweeping from left to right. The ground's so uneven, I have to keep glancing down at my feet. My skin crawls. My guts churn. Again I sense I'm being watched. Could that be Carver? No. He's like a wounded bull, not a hunting weasel. If he was close, I'd hear him. Or smell him. Or see fresh signs.

The river's barely running. Two rills in my path are narrow enough to step over. And between them, in the mud: Carver's footprints. Plain as day.

He's tracked the mud across a bed of dry cobbles, up to the top of a large rock and down the other side. So has a wild dog—more recently than Carver. A wavering line in the mud tells me Carver was dragging a musket. He must have been using it as a walking stick. He kept leaning on it—here, and here, and again over here. When he reached the far bank he grabbed a branch to steady himself and broke it. There's a hair caught in this bark where he rested his head.

He was feeling so poorly he could hardly stand. Any minute now, I'm expecting to stumble on his lifeless body. Surely he couldn't have walked much further?

But he did. He kept going. He pissed on this tree; the smell is still sharp. Then he plunged into the bush, right here, snapping sticks and scattering petals. The trail swerves where he changed direction. Why did he do that? Why turn left?

'What are you up to?' I mutter.

He's helped me by moving onto soft ground. There are footprints ahead—and paw-prints as well. The stock of a musket scraped against stone, leaving a brown mark. Deep dents show him leaning heavily on the gun, again and again, as he stooped to pass beneath a half-fallen tree. I duck under the same tree and emerge into a small clearing with a jumble of boulders in the middle.

Careful, Tom. Dropping behind a tea-tree, I squint at the rocky outcrop, which is pierced by a modest, low-set cave. Carver could be in there. Anything could. I'm seeing a trail, but I don't quite—

Yes I do. I understand now. Snapped branches: big, thick, leafy branches, taken from different sides of the same bush.

Carver broke them off deliberately, then dragged 'em behind him towards the rocks, sweeping away his tracks as he went. But was he thinking about his tracks? Or did he want the branches for another reason?

Bedding, perhaps? Did he sleep in that cave?

Is he sleeping there still?

Dry leaves have fallen across the scuff marks left by his branches; I count at least ten. And bird tracks, two sets of 'em. Those marks of his were made hours ago.

Bent double, clutching my carbine, I begin to circle the clearing until I'm directly behind the cave. From here I'll be able to climb onto the big slab of rock that forms its roof. Carver won't see me if I approach him from the rear. But he might hear me if I'm not very, very careful.

Quietly now. One step. Two steps. As soon as I reach the rock, it gets easier; all the leaves and sticks have tumbled off its sloping flank, which juts out of the dirt like the bow of a half-sunk ship. In my sheepskin soles I pad up and up, towards the far end of the rock. And when I reach the edge, I peer over it.

The cave's just beneath me. But is Carver inside?

Another thorn-beak squeaks an alarm. God grant Carver doesn't know that bird for a sentinel. Folk rarely do; they overlook bird calls. There can be grand battles and great love stories playing out overhead, and if you remark on it to someone like Joe, he'll just stare at you, blank-faced.

This bird doesn't like me. I flick a small twig in its direction and it flutters away, startled. Then I turn my attention back to the cave, shifting my grip on the carbine as I crane my neck for a look at the dark hole where Carver may—or may not—be hiding.

If he is in there, he's not making a sound.

Reaching for a pebble, I balance it carefully on the edge of the rock, place my foot next to it and aim my gun-muzzle straight down. If I kick the pebble, and it lands near the cave, Carver might come out to look. And if he does, I'll have a good, clean—

Christ!

A peck on my scalp, a flurry of wings—the thorn-beak's diving at me. I flap it away. Lose my balance. Tip over the edge.

Fall.

I land on the churned-up dirt at the mouth of the cave.

—++—

I'd been a month on Mr Barrett's farm when three troopers rode up to the front door. They were tracking a couple of bolters called Riley and Milgate. Though none of us had seen the missing pair, we were closely questioned by the troopers, who were condescending to Mr Barrett and very rough with his assigned men. They shouted, sneered and threatened to flog us if we didn't tell 'em what we knew. It was plain they thought all lags were liars.

They had a black with 'em called Sammy. He wore English clothes and had a good supply of chewing tobacco. The troopers were using him to track Riley and Milgate; he'd been on their trail for thirty miles. But when Mr Barrett asked if Sammy had tracked the runaways to his farm, the troopers wouldn't answer. They rode off quickly, taking Sammy with 'em.

'Came here to cadge a drink, I'll wager, and ignored the black's advice,' Mr Barrett later remarked. He also observed that to mounted police, all convicts were in cahoots, secretly supplying aid to other lags who might have hooked it. 'You'd have to be dead on the ground at their feet before they'd believe you hadn't absconded,' he said to George Trumble.

I learned two things, that day. I learned that no English poacher could compete with the likes of Sammy when it came to long-distance tracking. Thirty miles over rough ground? I'd never heard of such a thing. A black tracker must have an eagle's eye and a dog's nose; I can't account for it otherwise. I thought I knew Ixworth and its coverts as well as I knew my own hands, but the blacks must know this country the way God knows it. They must know every leaf and grain of soil.

I also learned that, no matter what a convict's situation might be, he'll never persuade a trooper that he's telling the truth. Once you've been shackled, you're a lag for life, whether you were sentenced to seven years or thirty.

That's why I'm trying not to think on the future. What hope is there that Carver won't take me down to hell with him? What hope is there that the troopers will believe a word I say? They'll likely hang me for the slaughter.

I'll have a better chance out here, despite the blacks and the snakes and the strangeness of everything.

✳

For one split second, I stare at the cave in front of me. Then I roll away.

That's when I notice the footprints. They're so faint I can see them only because my poor, battered nose is almost pressed against the ground.

They're leading out of the cave, not into it.

I know that tread. I know that gait. Those are Carver's tracks, though he wasn't leaning on his gun when he made 'em. He left the cave some time this morning, heading north. Towards the road or the farm?

If he was going back to the farm, he'd have made a sharp left turn and headed due west. It's the road he wanted.

A wise man would have dragged those leafy branches behind him to disguise his trail. But Carver must have left 'em where he slept—and now I can follow every step he took because the marks are quite fresh, with no leaves or paw-prints scattered over 'em and no drops of blood either. He wasn't bleeding, though he was ill. Look at the way he staggered when the bush proved too dense. Look at the way he grabbed that overhead bough and broke it off. Did he use it to beat his way through the undergrowth? I think he did. There are white splinters on the ground.

I'm keeping an eye on the sun as well as the trail. It seems to me Carver was executing a great half-circle, edging around the boundary of the farm as he made his way nor'west. This is where he stopped to spit. This is where his eye-patch caught on a twig and he lost it—or threw it away.

Every few yards I pause to listen, but I can't hear any snapping or rustling in the distance. If he's ahead of me somewhere, there's a good half-mile between us. Either that or he's not moving.

Careful now, Tom. What if he's lying in wait? Or what if someone else is? I'm still sensing someone on my trail—someone small and dark and silent. I thought I glimpsed a shadow out of the corner of my eye.

Unless I'm going mad?

A laughing jackass overhead mocks my efforts. There's cleared land through the trees ahead; that bright, distant sunshine could be the road. Have I reached it already?

Yes, I have. I even recognise this stretch of it. To my left, as I peer around a tree trunk, is Mr Barrett's house: a little grey box at the end of a pale, dusty drive. The house is so far away that I can't even make out the shape of the windows, but I know Rowdy's in there with nothing between him and Carver but a few animal traps and an unloaded pistol. *God, God, God. What am I going to do?* Where's Carver?

He's not by the house. He's not on the road. I study the sweep of the sandy cart track to my right as it disappears around a gentle curve. Surely he wouldn't have gone that way? It heads north, back towards the shepherds' hut.

Could he have decided to go to town instead?

Whatever he did, I won't know until I've checked the road for tracks. But that's going to leave me badly exposed. If he's trying to flush me, I'm in trouble.

Quick, then. Startle him. Burst out like a grouse.

I jump onto the road. Scan the dirt. Spot a footprint—and another, pointing away from the farm.

'What are you doing?' I whisper.

Why would he want to go north? He burned down the hut; there'd be no supplies left in it. Could he be hoping to find a sheep? Or did he hide something important back there?

No. Of course.

That stretch of road passes the meadow where Rowdy left Woodbine. He came back for me without the horse, so Carver must have known she was somewhere close by. Somewhere within easy reach of a wounded man. Somewhere with space enough for a large beast. But was it just Woodbine Carver wanted, or me as well?

If he had any sense he'd have taken the horse and gone. I doubt he has, though. *No witnesses.* He'll be watching Woodbine, waiting for me to come and fetch her.

Better to stay off the road.

That dirt track would be quieter than crashing through the forest, but Carver's likely guarding the meadow's entrance— in which case he'll spot me if I don't have cover. So I keep to the bush along the edge of the road, taking care where I put my feet, avoiding dry leaves and stems. Every once in a while I stop and close my eyes, listening hard. The first time I do this, I hear only the wind in the treetops. The second time, I hear a horse snorting.

Woodbine. She must be close.

Slowly I part the branches in front of me. Slowly I creep forward, duck under low boughs, step across fallen logs. Whenever I'm jabbed or scratched, I swallow my hiss of pain. Whenever my sleeve catches on a thorn, I stop. Ease back. Remove it with care.

The blacks have been here recently. Someone's been digging for roots. I sniff the air for smoke, but there's nothing.

At last I reach the edge of the meadow, which has been hacked out of thick forest by the side of the road. Where the trees used to be there is now only grass dotted with cross-cut stumps and a few frail saplings. Woodbine stands in the middle of this clearing, tied to one of the stumps. She's grazing half-heartedly, flicking the flies away with her tail. Her right saddlebag isn't bulging the way it used to. It looks as if someone has emptied it, leaving one of the straps unfastened.

I sink to my haunches behind a tree and survey the open space, searching for Carver. He must be here. But the meadow is surrounded on three sides by a wall of dense brush. If he's skulking behind it, he's as invisible to me as I must be to him. Will I have to sit and wait until he coughs or sneezes? What if I cough before he does?

I'm considering my options when a faint, nagging sound intrudes on my thoughts—the sound of a thorn-beak crying its alarm. I didn't notice it at first: the bird isn't anywhere near me. Its shrill piping is coming from across the meadow, way over there. And whatever's troubling it isn't moving.

The call rings out again and again, but no other bird responds. No other bird flaps out of the tree-tops.

I wonder if...?

Let's take a look.

Once again I set off, circling the meadow from south to north. I keep well back in the trees so Carver won't spy any leaves shaking or branches swaying. Every step is carefully measured, for all that I'm downwind of Carver. He won't hear me unless I accidentally fire my gun.

A crash, a thump, a flash of grey fur and a small kangaroo bounds off into the bush. I have to stop for a moment and gulp down some air. My breathing is unsteady. My pulse is racing. I'm sweating like a pig.

Keep at it, Tom. Not long now.

That bird is still peeping. It's so close, I decide to get down and stay down. At first I shuffle. Then I crawl. That's why, after advancing about thirty yards, I spy the ants.

They're small black ants, hurrying along in single file— and each is carrying a tiny white bundle. A breadcrumb? A grain of sugar? There was sugar in Woodbine's saddle-bags. Carver must have taken it. He must have taken the bread, too.

He can't be far away.

That thorn-beak is just overhead. I can hear it. I can smell sweat and black powder. The muffled rasp of laboured breathing is interrupted, now and again, by the sound of someone chewing with an open mouth.

Inch by inch, I raise my head. Inch by inch, I turn it.

And there he is. Dan Carver.

Sitting with his back to me, gazing out over the meadow.

15

I WAS alone in the house when my brother came home for the last time.

It was just after daybreak. My father was out in the coverts somewhere; he never told me where he went, any more than he would have told the dogs or the fire-irons. I was roused from my sleep by a knock at the front door, and opened it to find a small crowd in the street. The vicar was there, with the parish constable and Colonel Newton's underkeeper.

Jack was there too. He was laid out on an old door under a bloodstained blanket.

'You must prepare yourself, Tom Clay,' the vicar said.

The next thing I remember we were all in the kitchen, with Jack lying on my father's bed. The parish constable was explaining that Jack's wounding had been an accident. ('He was where he should not have been—in the line of fire.') They'd shot Jack's dog, Savage, after he attacked the colonel's gamekeeper. This second blow, on top of the first, left me speechless. I stood in a corner and watched the local authorities commandeer our house.

But then my father came home. His sack was empty, so he must have heard all the voices and dumped his catch outside. When he walked through the kitchen door, everyone else fell silent. He was the only armed man in the room.

'Richard Clay,' said the vicar, 'you must prepare yourself—'

My father's gun was loaded. He half-cocked it and said, 'Get out.'

I'll swear to this day, it wasn't the musket that dispersed the men in our kitchen. It was the look on my father's face. It sent the underkeeper fleeing, and the vicar and curate along with him. A farrier called Styles held his ground, along with Colley the blacksmith and the parish constable—until my father took a step forward and said, through his blackened teeth, 'Was it Clegg?'

The constable opened his mouth, then thought better of speaking. He nodded instead.

'Tell him he's a dead man,' my father continued, quite calmly. 'Tell him no matter where he goes, no matter what he does, I'll always be on his trail. He'll never have another moment's peace while he's living—and that won't be long. You tell him that.'

This was the baldest truth ever spoken. Clegg was in his grave by the month's end, having been stalked like a hind before the final shot finished him. I don't know if that shot came with a warning, but I doubt it. A poacher's greatest weapon is stealth.

You'd be a fool to warn anyone who's bigger or quicker or better armed than you are.

⧺

Carver sits on a fallen log, hunched and bloody and ragged. On the ground to his left lies the duelling pistol. To his right he's placed a musket where he can reach it easily. He's nursing his other musket, which is probably cocked; I can't see the hammer from here, so I'm not sure. If I were Carver, I would have cocked it.

Tucked against the log, just under his rump, is a half-opened cloth bundle leaking supplies: a round of cheese, a hunk of mutton, a tin of tea, a bag of sugar. The sugar-bag is slightly split. That's why the ants are raiding it.

He's watching the horse. I knew he would be. He's skulking behind a screen of foliage, waiting for me to approach Woodbine so he can shoot me dead. Every so often he bites into a heel of bread, tears off a mouthful, chews, swallows.

As the crumbs rain down, the ants pick 'em up.

Peep-peep-peep. Though the thorn-beak above him is becoming more and more frantic, he pays no heed to its piping and fluttering. Good. He's so fixed on the horse that his ears aren't tuned to the noises around him.

I need to line up my shot, but I can't do it down here. I have to stand. So I shuffle sideways—very slowly and very, very quietly—until my swollen nose is almost pressed against the bark of a big white gum tree covered in scribbles. The tree is so wide that it blocks my view of Carver. Pray God it blocks his view of me.

I'm holding my breath as I straighten my knees, sliding up the tree trunk until I'm finally standing. Once on my feet, I begin to adjust my grip on the carbine, inch by cautious inch. Carver coughs. Then he groans. His ribs must be hurting him.

When he coughs again, I cock my gun. Now I just have to aim it.

I'll wait until the next gust of wind. In a forest full of tossing, nodding branches, Carver may not spy a gun barrel emerging from behind a tree. He's not looking this way, but there's no telling what he might glimpse from the corner of his eye.

The sight of the food makes my mouth water. I'm glad I ate this morning, else my stomach would be growling like a mastiff. Carver chews slowly and doggedly. His breathing is laboured. The coat he's wearing is so stiff with blood you could break it across your knee.

And here's a puff of wind. The bush sways and dances around me. Leaves rustle. Boughs creak. I raise the carbine and point it at Carver's back.

Now.

For a moment I feel dizzy; the muzzle wavers. How am I going to do this? To shoot a man in the back—to shoot him in cold blood—is wicked. A sin. Will I go to heaven if I kill Dan Carver? What if Gyp's waiting for me there, and I never arrive?

Our Father, who art in heaven, hallowed be thy name...

I take a deep breath and pull the trigger.

It's a flash in the pan.

Carver spins around, wildly firing his musket, but I'm already running and I'm faster than he is. Oh God, oh God, he's got three guns. I duck as he shoots again. The ball smacks off a nearby tree. A branch slaps me in the face and the bush is so dense that it tugs at my clothes and they rip.

Carver fires. The ball sends up a spurt of dust.

Three shots. He has to reload now and I'm well ahead; if I can increase the distance and stay in thick scrub I might lose him.

Please God...

My foot drops into a hidden hole and I go crashing, rolling along the ground. I drop the carbine—leap to my feet again—snatch up the gun and away I go. I can hear Carver lumbering along behind me. I can hear him gasping for breath. God help us, is that sun up ahead? Am I making for the meadow?

I can't be. I'm well past the meadow. This must be another, smaller clearing but the scrub is the only thing keeping me alive. Once Carver can see me—once he has a clear line of sight—

His next shot whizzes past and I duck and drop, plunging into a tangle of tightly matted undergrowth about four feet high. It scrapes my face and tweaks my hair and tears my clothes, but I'm past caring. This is my only chance. I'm not a hare. I'm not a sheep. I have to start thinking like a hunter.

I turn my carbine around so that I'm holding it like a club.

'I'm going to drive you out, you little bastard!' Carver cries hoarsely. He fires into the thicket, then begins to crunch through it. Suddenly he stops. Paper rattles.

He's reloading again.

'You always thought you was sharper than me,' he continues, gasping and wheezing, 'but that ain't why you're a dead man, Tom Clay.'

The sound of the ramrod tells me he's just a few yards away. But I can't reach him. I can't see him. All I can see are twigs and nuts and leaves and flowers—and the big, red ants marching across the ground in front of me, just a few inches from my boots. Ants like that will bite like dogs, and there's nothing I can do to stop 'em running up my leg if they've a mind to. A single movement will show Carver where I'm hiding. I can't risk that.

'You know why you're a dead man? Because you thought yer *dog* was sharper than me,' Carver continues. More paper. More tamping. He's loading another gun. 'I hope yer dog died slow, Tom Clay,' he croaks. He's coming closer. 'I hope it squealed like a rat. I hope you had to break its bloody neck to put it out of its misery.'

A gun fires. That was close. I can smell the black powder. He's stopped to reload again; rip, tap, scrape, click.

A gust of wind shakes the bushes. My heartbeat is making my hands tremble. *Please, God…please, God…please, please, please…*

'When I'm finished with you,' Carver growls, 'I'm going to find what's left o' that dog, and cut off its ears, and pull out its teeth and wear 'em.'

There. Just a glimpse of his legs passing a few feet away, and—

A gun explodes overhead as I slam the butt of my carbine into the back of his good knee.

He pitches forward. His pistol goes flying and he lands on his face, flattening the bushes beneath him.

I jump up and grab the pistol and fire, but nothing happens. It isn't loaded. So I hurl it off into the bush, as far as I can throw it, and raise my carbine over the back of Carver's head. I'm about to ram the stock down onto his skull when he grabs my ankle. He yanks and I fall, dropping my gun as I hit the ground. Before I can get away, he seizes a handful of my hair.

I'm screaming, I can't help it. I flail at him but when I hit out I don't connect. He rolls over onto his back, dragging me with him. Tears spurt from my eyes. Then he clamps his forearm across my throat so I'm pinned to his chest.

He starts squeezing.

I claw at his arm and kick at his legs but his hold only tightens. I stretch and lunge and grope for my carbine, until the tips of my straining fingers brush against its smooth stock. But Carver shoves it aside with his free hand.

'Oh no you don't,' he grunts.

I can't breathe. *I can't breathe.* He's pressing harder. My eyes feel as if they're about to pop from my head. Frantically my hand flails about, reaching for something—anything—a stick. A stick.

'I could do this to yer spine,' he grunts in my ear. 'Snap it in two.'

My fingers close on the stick and then I feel something else underneath it. Sand. Big, coarse grains of sand piled up around a little hole. The ants' nest.

With my last ounce of strength I jab my stick into that hole and keep jabbing, again and again. I want the ants out. I want 'em swarming. I want 'em spitting mad.

'We're going to have some fun when you wake up,' says Carver. The dark's closing in, but I can't let it—not yet—my lungs are bursting, my neck's breaking, my head's spinning...

Carver yelps and flinches. Then he loosens his grip to flap at something on his ear.

I snap to attention.

My vision clears just as he roars, 'Little *bastards*,' and I know the ants have got him. I know it even before I swing my legs up over his head in a neat backflip, breaking his hold. Over I go. Perfect roll.

I scoop up my carbine and dive into the bush.

⊬

The last time I was caught, a gamekeeper kicked my legs out from under me. He came up behind me in the pouring rain, clapped his hand on my shoulder and knocked me to the ground. Then he took my brace of pheasants and put a gun to my head.

The pheasants weren't for my dinner. I'd been planning to sell 'em. After Jack was killed and my father was hanged, I had no livelihood. No trade. All I had was poaching. It was that or the workhouse—and no one ever gets out of the workhouse alive.

I was sent to the same gaol where my father had been held six months earlier. I knew what to expect when I arrived because I'd called on him there, just once, before they hanged him. Bury gaol is a foul den but no worse than the *Lord Lyndoch*. At least the floor of a prison stays firm under your feet.

My father didn't hit me when I told him I'd brought no food. (I'd barely enough to feed myself at the time.) Instead he asked me about his new dog, Pontius. I told him the dog was well. Then he asked me about Colonel Newton's latest underkeeper. I told him the latest underkeeper was sly, but not such a bully as Clegg or Cocksedge.

My father said it was strange I hadn't fallen to the game-keeper's gun; he had always expected it. My brother had been more skilled, yet the keeper had done for him. It made no sense.

I said nothing.

My father rambled on about the other coves in his cell, the clergyman who kept bothering him, the cruelty of his gaolers, the ignorance of his judge. He chastised me for not bringing Pontius. He didn't ask me how I was faring on my own. I don't think he cared.

He told me to come to the hanging with his friends from the Mackerel's Eye and see how a man of courage met his fate, but I didn't. I had no wish to. And for once I knew I wouldn't be punished if I disobeyed.

I did see two folk hanged at Bury gaol while I was there. The gaol had a great stone gatehouse with a flat roof, and the hangings took place on that roof, in full view of the crowds gathered outside. Those inside were also marshalled to watch the proceedings, which many of the prisoners enjoyed very much. The governor employed the famous hangman William Calcraft on both occasions. A great cheer went up when Calcraft grabbed the restless legs of both dangling men and pulled down firmly. He does this to break necks, I'm told, but it has become such a habit with him that the crowds feel cheated when he doesn't.

Calcraft hanged my father—and my father, I heard, was granite to the end. This was no great comfort to me then, and it isn't now. My father lived hard and died hard, and would scorn me for doing less. I don't doubt that he would have admired Dan Carver's endurance.

I know he would have thought Dan Carver the better man.

+++

I'm running. My throat hurts. My scalp burns where Carver yanked out my hair, but he must be feeling worse than I am. Surely he can't stay on his feet for much longer?

I gasp for breath as I beat at the brush with my carbine— and here's the clearing I wanted to avoid. The fallen tree that made it is a monster, wider than a ship's mast and longer than a steeple. Shall I climb over it or go around?

Climb over; its bulk will shield me when I'm on the other side, please God. The bark's rough, so there's no end of footholds. Hand over hand, up to the top and—

A gunshot. *Christ.* I slip down the other side and land, winded. Something's wrong. My hand—my left hand—I'm looking at the third finger and it's not there. It's gone from the first knuckle up, blood spurting, pain welling. *Pain*. But I can't stop; I have to run. Grab the wound. Hold on tight.

Sweet Jesus, it hurts. It's white-hot agony. The carbine thumps against my back as I stumble back into the bush. He'll follow the blood. Should I stop to bind the stump? I can't. I can't stop.

No need for silence now—not if he can follow my blood trail. Fast and noisy wins the race. But I'm gut-sick and the pain is like a hammer and I trip, stagger, fall; the jolt nearly kills me.

He's still coming. I can hear him.

Up again, teeth clenched. *Go, Tom. Keep moving*. Arm's numb, hand feels molten. I'm dizzy and there's blood everywhere.

The next shot's wide; it loses itself in the scrub. And now I'm back at the cave but I can't hide in there, I'll be cornered. He's bound to find me. As I pass its dark mouth, I notice dog tracks. Fresh.

What if...?

One flick of my fingers leaves a spatter of blood near the entrance to the cave. It might delay Carver, at least for a minute. He might stop to check whether I'm inside. Meanwhile, I'm retracing my route back to the farm. Out of the clearing. Under the half-fallen tree. Keep going. Keep going. I'm getting wobbly—have to stop for an instant and lean against the nearest tree to catch my breath. I'm all pain. There's nothing else.

None of Pa's beatings was ever this bad.

I push myself off a shaggy tree trunk and stagger forward, trying to concentrate on the marks left behind by Carver— the snapped twigs, the loose threads, the dents, the scratches. I didn't leave much of a trail myself when I passed this way before. I should be proud of that. No footsteps to speak of, thanks to the fleece on my soles. No black hairs. No smashed bushes.

No blood.

Another shot rings out. I flinch, but not because it was close. Did Carver just fire into the cave? I think so. I hope so. He's lagging behind…

And here's the river: good. Instead of following Carver's tracks, I splash upstream a few yards—I've a goal in mind now, and there's a quicker route to it than the one I took when I was tracking Carver. I can't stay here, though; I need to be in the bush. I'm like a hare in a field on this riverbed.

But I can hardly think through the pain—and the smooth, tumbled rocks are treacherous when you're dizzy. The water carries my blood away. That'll break the trail, though not for long. Blood spills onto the boulders as I haul myself over 'em, back into the forest.

I'm feeling faint—tired—and nearly fall over a dead sheep before I smell it. How did I miss that stench? I know the sheep; she's from Barrett's farm. A wild dog must have savaged her.

I stumble past, trying not to look. Birds call in the canopy. Down by the river, Carver's cough is faint enough to give me a little courage. He's slowing.

So am I.

Not far now. Gyp's grave is somewhere up ahead. When I reach the paddock, I'll reach the grave. Please, Gyp, watch over me. All I need is time: a few minutes. I'm muddled and light-headed and…lost? Have I wandered off course?

No. Here's a lopped tree. And another. And another. The forest is thinning. The unfiltered sun beats down. Here's a dry apple core, a white thread, a boot-mark stamped into a patch of dried mud.

Here's…

A black.

A young one. Half-hidden by dappled shade.

I freeze. We stare at each other. He's still as a rock, wiry and beardless and wrapped in a hide cloak. The spear in his hand isn't pointed at me.

His eyes gleam like water in a well. They flick towards my crippled hand. I don't know what to do. Run? Shoot? Roar?

I can't run; I haven't the strength. I can't shoot; my gun's not loaded. And if I shout, Carver will hear me.

I've never been this close to a black. The top of his chest is scarred, but the scars are so regular they must be deliberate. His hair curls like mine. He's wearing a bone necklace.

A strange expression flickers over his smooth, dark face. I don't know what it means. He doesn't look angry, or wary, or scared. Is it confusion?

Pity?

Then he retreats, fading slowly back into the shadowy bush. He barely makes a sound, no more than a snake or a bird. If he wanted to kill me I'd be dead by now. I must be safe. Safe from him, at least. Not from Carver.

I stagger forward, wondering if I have the strength to go on. But here's the tree by Gyp's grave; there's no mistaking it. I chose it for its sturdy branches and the dense bush that almost rings its base. The only clear patch beneath it lies directly in front of the footholds that I cut into its speckled trunk yesterday.

I wipe my hand across the hatchet scars and leave a wavering smear of blood. That should do. Now—where to hide?

Over there. *Quick.*

When Mr Barrett first cleared the southern paddock, he left great piles of felled logs that he burned down to ash and charcoal. One of the piles stands near Gyp's grave, sunken and compressed and tufted with green but still a big, grey lump pierced by jagged black shapes. Dropping to my knees, I crawl towards this ash-heap through the long grass, one-handed. The other hand is pressed hard against my belly; if I leave a blood trail, I'm dead. But the pain of the pressure... God help us. *Thepainthepainthepainthepain...*

As I pass Gyp's grave I try to distract myself, thinking about how she always protected me and how I've been trying to protect her. I didn't want Carver digging her up. I took measures to stop him from taking his revenge. I thought I'd be long gone when Carver finally arrived at this place.

I was wrong.

When I reach the ash-heap I shuffle around behind it. Now it lies between me and the grave. Beyond the grave stands the marked tree; up in the tree, barely visible from where I'm squatting, is a patch of grubby white linen.

I wish I had some linen now. I need to bind my hand, but I can't tear a strip off my shirt in case Carver hears me. I can hear him; he's crashing through the bush, heading in this direction. I don't have much time.

The carbine slides from my shoulder onto the ground. Quickly I shrug off my coat and wrap it around my injured arm. I have to bite my lip to stop myself from whimpering. Sweat stings my eyes; I'm shaking like someone with a fever.

A coating of ash might disguise me, but if I stir up the fine grey powder it'll drift into the air like smoke.

There he is. Lurching out of the shade, a musket in each hand, dark, bloody, misshapen—a corpse walking. God ha' mercy.

He's seen the blood on the tree. His head jerks up. He steps back and drops one gun as he raises the other, peering at the branches above him.

He's glimpsed what I left up there. I know he has.

'Remember what I told you about that native bear?' he says hoarsely, circling the bushes at the base of the tree. At last he reaches the gap in this ragged hedge; if he steps forward, he'll have a clear shot at the stuffed shirt that I dragged up the tree yesterday evening, just before I dug Gyp's grave. From below, the bundle looks like someone huddled in a woody fork, shoulders hunched, head tucked down. I was so careful putting it up there. I nearly fell, making sure I got it right. Rowdy thought me mad but I was afraid for Gyp.

I chose this site because of the tree.

'You don't learn, do you, Tom Clay?' Carver wheezes. Every step is so heavy you'd swear it was his last. He moves as if he's carrying a horse on his back, gasping for breath, limping towards the trunk. His eyes are on the canopy. One step. Two—

The ground breaks beneath his foot and he screams as the trap beneath him springs shut.

He drops his gun. Grabs the jaws that are clamped around his calf. *Now*, Tom! I should be sprinting but I'm stumbling instead, reeling towards him across the grass. He has his back to me. I'm closing in.

I'm nearly there.

He's still screaming and it masks my approach. His hands move from the jaws of the trap to the chain, then to the peg, but I sharpened the peg and hammered it through a root. He'll not get it out.

I reach his gun. I jerk it away. Aim it. Cock it.

He hears the click and swings around, suddenly speech-less.

'You're the one who doesn't learn,' I tell him. Dangling a bait above a trap? It must be the oldest trick in the world.

His jagged teeth are bared. His breath hisses through them—short, sharp gusts of pain. His one eye is fixed on the muzzle of the gun wavering in the air just a few feet from his head. I'm trying to prop it on the coat wadded around my left hand, but the weight is too much. I can't keep it still.

All the same, I won't miss. Not from this distance.

I've never shot a man. Look at him: his good eye is a bulging red ball. His face is purple and grey—caked with blood—twisted—inhuman. I'd be putting him out of his misery. Do I want to do that?

'You think you can break me?' he croaks. 'You want me to beg? You won't break me. I'll never beg. I'm flint. Granite.'

He's mad. Mad and half-dead. He's finished.

Slowly I lower my weapon. Then I take one step back, lift my head and howl like a wild dog.

'You won't escape!' he rasps as I start to retreat. 'I'll come for you!'

Ignoring him, I go to pick up the other musket. It's unloaded. I wonder if he's run out of cartridges.

A real dog wails in the distance. How far away? About a hundred yards? I didn't realise they were so close.

The chain jangles wildly as Carver shakes it, trying to pull out the peg.

'You'd better run, Tom Clay!' he gasps.

I'm not going to run. I can't run. I don't have the strength.

Another dog yaps and whines somewhere in the trees. It sounds troubled. It'll be coming to investigate soon.

More groaning. More jingling. Doubtless Carver's trying to free himself but I don't look back to make sure. With a musket slung over each shoulder, I retrieve my carbine from the ash-heap.

Behind me, a dog growls.

'Get!' Carver cries. 'Get out of it!'

Still I don't look back. This time Carver won't be running away. This time he's met his match. I don't have to linger here anymore.

Instead I make for the house across the paddock, dizzy but with hope in my heart. I can see a way forward now

—just a glimpse—and I want to share it with Rowdy Cavanagh.

Behind me are noises I have to block out. So I raise my voice.

'Rowdy?' I yell. 'It's me.' Walking away from the scuffles and snarls, I busy myself with plans for the future. Why not take Mr Barrett's flour and tea, and some guns and blankets, and flee into the bush? Rowdy and I could sleep in caves and snare wild beasts. We could eat berries and roots. The settlers who'd see our fires would probably think us blacks and ignore us. The blacks who'd see our fires would probably think us Carver, and stay away.

I could tame a wild dog pup. One day. Perhaps.

The wild dogs behind me are bickering now. I don't want to know why; I wish I could block my ears but my hand's too sore. I'm queasy, parched, light-headed. I need to sleep. To heal. We should have time enough for that, before the troopers come. With meat and laudanum and shelter we'll have a fair chance. What's a finger, after all? My father lost an eye and was none the worse for it.

Here's the kitchen where Gyp died. I pause for a moment to prop myself against a wall.

I feel so ill. I can still hear Carver.

'*Rowdy!*' I yell.

No reply. I stumble forward, past the winter chard, the turnip beds and the bean-stakes, until finally I reach the back stairs. I'm tottering like a drunkard; should I risk the trap I laid?

I'll have to. The front door's even better defended.

'*Rowdy!*'

Still no answer. Carefully I step over the middle stair, knowing there's a bear trap underneath. When I'm stronger I'll have to move that. Will I have time to carve Gyp a headboard before we go? Will I have strength enough to bury those poor souls in the cool-room?

The pain is like a brand. I've never felt anything to match it.

'Rowdy?'

The back door squeaks open. It's very quiet. When I reach the bedroom I lean against the door-jamb to husband my strength.

Rowdy is lying in bed. He's not moving. His head's turned away from me.

'Rowdy, wake up.'

He doesn't even twitch. I sense it before I know it. The whimper I hear must be mine—it can't be his.

No. Rowdy...

As I reach him, my knees buckle. I have to grab the bedframe with one hand; the other's just a ball of pain. Propped against the footboard, I give him a shove. And again, hard. But he doesn't wake.

He's still warm.

'Please. *Rowdy.*' He can't have left me.

I shake him. I hit him. I scream in his ear. It changes nothing.

I've lost my friend. I've lost my flock.

I'm all alone.

Epilogue

IT'S AS well Rowdy died in a soft bed. If he hadn't, I would have given him those orange berries. He'd be lying beside me now, his guts turned to water, dying slowly in the dirt just as I am. I wouldn't want his death on my conscience. I didn't even kill Carver, in the end. I didn't kill anyone.

Will that help me when I face judgement? Maybe it means I'll see Rowdy again. And Ma. And Gyp. I miss 'em all, especially Gyp.

Leaves crunch; my eyes snap open.

I'm too weak to lift my head, but I know he's there. A black. I can see his dusty ankles, the base of his spear, the trailing hem of his cloak.

He says something in his language. Then he drops to his haunches beside me, still speaking.

It's the same black. The beardless one.

He picks up a berry and thrusts it under my nose. Then he splits the fruit and removes the black seed, still chattering. Tosses the seed. Scoops out the white flesh. Discards the skin.

The flesh goes into his mouth. He waves his hand: he's lecturing me. Should I not have eaten the seed, then? Should I not have eaten the skin?

He rises again and moves away. Did he take my gun? My flour? At least he didn't take my blanket. I don't begrudge the gun or the flour, but only a savage would deprive a dying man of his blanket.

Now that he's gone, I can die in peace. The pain in my gut's settled. I'm desert-dry, but my water-bag's drained and I haven't the strength to refill it. The thirst keeps dragging me back here, to this empty wilderness. Otherwise I could fall asleep and dream myself to death.

Footsteps. He's back, and making no bones about it. Muttering to himself. Snapping branches. I can't see what he's doing, but I have to. I have to see.

Feebly I roll onto my back, squinting. There he is, over by that stump. He's put a wooden vessel on the ground and is squatting beside it, his fingers working away at...something. He's kneading the stuff in his hands. Dropping it into the bowl. Glancing in my direction to scold me, his voice impatient. What have I done? How have I caused offence? I've killed no one. Stolen nothing. He dusts off his hands, motions with one, then rubs his belly with the other. I don't understand what he's trying to say.

No, no, I can't. I'm too tired. Too ill. Can't hold my head up...or my eyelids...The sun's on my face and all I can see is red...

But now I'm swimming out of the crimson dark and someone is shaking me. It's him—the black. His face is close to mine.

His eyes are huge; there's a fly on his cheek. He tucks a hand under my head and says something. I know it's a question.

'What...don't...' My voice is a thin creak. My throat is lined with sand. He's holding his vessel to my lips, and there's water in it. *Water.* Fragments of red gum soaking in a pool of water.

He tips the water onto my tongue.

Ugh, it's bitter. But he won't let me turn my head away. He forces the drink down, tipping the vessel higher and higher until it's clunking against my front teeth. The taste's not so bad once you get used to it.

When I've finished every last drop, he lays my head back down and grins—a crooked grin like Rowdy's, but cleaner. More joyful. He talks like Rowdy too, on and on, pulling faces and motioning with his hands.

He's telling me a story. There's a gun in the story, because he shoots it. There's a tall tree and a wild dog. I know there's a wild dog because he throws back his head and howls like one. Then he laughs until there are tears in his eyes.

Is he telling *my* story?

At the end of the story he ruffles my hair and stands again. I follow him with my eyes. He's emptied my pack all over the ground: everything's laid out neatly. My tea caddy. My sugar tin. My safety matches.

He's lit a fire. For me. Two dead fish lie beside it.

When he points at the fish and speaks, I nod.

'Fish,' I say, and he smiles again.

It's a good enough beginning.